# ONE LAST BREATH

## S.C. STOKES

PRESCIENT PUBLISHING

# CONTENTS

# CHAPTER 1

The door shattered inward, the chain providing scant resistance as the entire door was blown off its hinges.

Kasey bolted upright, rubbing her face, trying to clear the sleep from her eyes. The fatigue of running from the Arcane Council had worn her down. Their agents were everywhere, an ever-present threat scouring the city.

For three days, and three restless nights, Kasey and Sanders had hopped from motel to motel, trying to stay one step ahead of their pursuers. They couldn't go home; they couldn't reach out to any known associates. The Ninth Precinct had been overrun by ADI agents masquerading as FBI agents. Kasey and Sanders had spent their first day on the run watching the station, only to see dozens of agents leave red-faced when they had come up empty handed.

The ADI, however, had not been deterred. They had simply stepped up their efforts and expanded their search.

Nowhere was safe. The resources of the entire Arcane Council had been deployed with the single purpose of running her down. Fortunately, with Sanders' extensive understanding of ADI protocols, they had managed to stay one step ahead of the ADI.

Until now.

Agents surged into the motel room. Their portable battering ram made short work of the door. Kasey rose from the bed, her lips forming the words for a spell that would evict them unceremoniously from the building.

That spell never made it off her lips.

The lead agent raised his weapon and fired at Kasey. She tumbled off the bed and hit the carpet hard. A sharp cracking sound informed her that her collar bone may have broken. She found herself gasping for air as she writhed in pain on the floor.

The lead agent raised his helmet. "Bean Bag rounds work a charm, don't they? Good luck casting a spell when you can't breathe, Miss Chase. Consider it payback for the Archives."

Kasey looked up and saw Kazinsky, smug grin in place.

"I...hate...you," Kasey mouthed.

"Cuff her, boys," Kazinsky declared.

Agents surged around him and buried Kasey in a mound of manpower. Squirming in their grasp, she kicked one man in the shins before headbutting a second agent, but the effort was futile. She was outnumbered dozens to one.

She winced in pain as she was rolled onto her stomach. Her arms were twisted behind her back before handcuffs were forced around her wrists with extreme prejudice.

She was hauled to her feet, dragged to the kitchen, and dumped in a chair.

Kazinsky pulled out a second chair in front of her and straddled it.

"Where is Sanders?" Kazinsky shouted, slapping the table.

"I dunno. Haven't seen him," Kasey lied, as a bead of sweat ran down her brow.

"Don't lie to me, Kasey! We know he checked into the motel. It was the front desk clerk that recognized him and phoned in the tip, so stop wasting my time and tell me where he is."

"Maybe he is in the bathroom. Have you checked in there?" she asked, leaning back in the chair. Sanders had left the motel hours ago, not giving up hope of rallying support against the Shinigami and his minions.

Kazinsky shook his finger at her. "I'm warning you, Kasey. My patience is running thin. If you tell us where Sanders is, the Council may show you leniency."

"Leniency." Kasey scoffed. Trapped and alone, Kasey's heart began to pound. "The chancellor has already pronounced my sentence. I'll not be telling you anything. So, good luck finding him on your own."

The furrow on Kazinsky's brow deepened. "Keep it up. Keep pushing me, Kasey. I might just carry out the sentence here and now."

"Do your worst," Kasey spat, squirming against the agent that held her down.

"Very well," Kazinsky replied. Standing up he drew his side arm. "I'm warning you, this one will be lethal."

Kasey let out an exhausted sigh. "We all die eventually. Now is as good a day as any."

Kazinsky lowered the weapon and pointed it at her face.

Kasey stared down the business end of Kazinsky's silver 9mm service weapon and hoped death would be swift.

As Kazinsky's finger tightened, a swirling gray mist descended, obscuring her vision. The kitchen faded from view, taking with it Kazinsky and his pistol. When the mist cleared, she found herself lying on her back on the motel bed, staring up at the ceiling.

*Phew. It was just a vision.*

Kasey sucked in a deep breath to calm her racing heart.

Looking up at the cracked ceiling plaster and the faded paint, Kasey knew the importance of her vision. The vision had taken place here, in the very room she now lay in.

*They are coming.*

Kasey rolled off the bed. In the commotion of her vision, she hadn't had the chance to notice the time. The ADI could arrive any minute.

She raced around the room and gathered her things, tossing them in a cheap duffel she had purchased the day before. Her unexpected flight from the ADI hadn't afforded her the luxury of being able to pack any supplies. What little they had, they had bought along the way.

In seconds, Kasey had gathered her meager possessions. Glancing at the front door, she thought better of leaving through that entrance. The ADI might be waiting for her even now. Instead, she made her way back into the bedroom and opened the window. It led to a fire escape that ran down the back of the motel. It was three floors down to the alley floor.

Kasey shimmied out the window and grabbed her duffel before sliding the window shut. Glancing around, she could see no sign of the ADI. Slinging the duffel over her shoulder, she raced down the ladder.

Her feet hit the second-floor landing, and, in two steps, she was on the next ladder making her way down to the ground level. As her shoes struck the asphalt, tires screeched to a halt in front of the motel.

Kasey raced to the edge of the alley and risked a glimpse around the corner of the building. Three black SUVs had pulled up out front. Agents piled out, already dressed in combat gear and ready for action.

*Not getting out of here that way.*

She looked down the alley in the other direction. It was a dead end. Her heart raced as the net closed in around her. Searching for a means of escape she found none, the alley bare but for a row of dumpsters for the motel's refuse.

As the commotion in front of the motel intensified, Kasey knew she was out of time. She ran to the dumpsters. The first was empty. The second was almost full to the brim.

Kasey fought back a retching sensation in the back of her throat as the dumpsters' stench enveloped her. A weeks' worth of room service and take away rotted in the trash.

She screwed up her nose, but she understood the alternative. She'd already watched it transpire. Kasey lifted the lid and leapt into the dumpster, taking care not to take too deep a breath for fear she would be ill. She considered herself to have a strong stomach but the stench was getting to her.

As quickly as she could, she rearranged the trash until she had burrowed down inside the dumpster, burying both herself and the duffel. With one hand, she pulled down the lid before easing the last few bags of trash over her. Someone could open the dumpster and stare right at her and, provided she didn't make a sound, she would not be detected. She settled in for an uncomfortable wait. Time was difficult to judge in the dumpster, so she settled in and did her best to distract herself from the stench of the surrounding trash.

A loud crack came from above.

*That'll be the door.*

She'd made it out in the nick of time. Even now, the agents would be crawling all over the motel room searching for any trace of her. At the thought of Kazinsky's inevitable frustration, Kasey couldn't help but smile. She hunkered down into the trash and did her best to remain as still as possible.

Not for the first time, she loathed the position she found herself stuck in. She was one of two people alive who knew that the Master of the Shinigami was masquerading as the head of the Arcane Council. In their ignorance, the ADI and council now pursued her with single-minded vigor, all the while oblivious to the traitor in their midst.

The attack on New York City drew nearer day by day. Masquerading as Arthur Ainsley, the Shinigami was free to move about as he pleased and bring their deadly plot to fruition.

Unfortunately, Kasey was too busy fleeing for her life to do anything about it. The ADI were not going to hear her out. In their flight from the Council Chambers, Kasey and Sanders had left more than a dozen of them in the Administorum and done untold damage to the Arcane Council's headquarters. It had been a necessity to escape, but one that had further aligned the community against them.

Kasey longed to turn the table on the Shinigami, but she could not see how that was possible. He hid himself behind a veritable army of ADI agents. Until they could confront him, it was the word of two wanted fugitives against the Chancellor of the Arcane Council. The last thing Kasey wanted was to give him notice that she knew his true identity. It was the ace up her sleeve and wasn't to be played until they were in a position to not only reveal him but take him out.

As Kasey pondered on her predicament, footsteps filled the alley. "Search it all," a voice rang out. "The clerk insists it's them. They have to be around here somewhere."

Kasey heard the first dumpster opened. Its steel lid let out a loud clang as it struck the brick wall behind it. Moments later, it slammed shut. Kasey startled at the impact.

Steeling herself, she drew in a short breath and held it. The dumpster she was in opened. Shafts of light streaked along the edges of the dumpster, and she only hoped that she had hidden herself well enough.

"You have to be kidding me." The agent's sniff turned into a dry retch before backing away from the dumpster. "They aren't in there, that's for sure."

He slammed the dumpster shut.

Kasey let out her breath and did her best to calm her racing heart.

Each of the dumpsters was opened and slammed in turn. Eventually, the agents completed their search and the footsteps faded to nothing.

It was early evening and the sun would be setting soon. Sanders' prolonged absence was making her nervous.

If not for her vision, Kasey might have feared him captured. Her vision gave her confidence that Sanders remained at large. Sanders had taken the burner phone with him, so she had to remain near the motel to rendezvous with him and warn him of the ADI's progress.

*Time to move again.* There would be no sleeping in the motel, though she was sorely tempted to try and sneak back into the room for a shower.

She thought better of the foolish notion; stinking was infinitely better than imminent death, which is what awaited her should the ADI catch up with her. Clearly one of the staff was a member of the magical community. Otherwise, they would have had no idea who Sanders was.

Word was spreading of the Director of the ADI who had gone rogue. The Shinigami was doing his best to deter the magical community from aiding the fugitives. Branding them as murderers and traitors had kept them isolated, and unfortunately, it had resulted in a phone call tipping off the ADI as to their whereabouts.

For a moment, Kasey daydreamed about what she would do if she ever caught up with the Master of the Shinigami. Her track record against their death cult was impressive, but she'd seen the Master in action against Sanders. He was a formidable wizard of indeterminate age. Who knew what he would do if cornered. He was willing to watch a city burn and a country devastated to carry out his purposes.

No, dealing with the Master of the Shinigami would require greater care and far more planning than Kasey was used to operating with. She just needed to survive long enough to figure it out.

She thanked her lucky stars that her vision had manifested when it had. Minutes later, and she would now be staring down the barrel of Kazinsky's pistol instead of wallowing in a dumpster full of trash.

As unpleasant as her current circumstances were, she knew only too well that it could be infinitely worse.

The peal of tires screeching out of the parking lot announced the departure of the ADI, but Kasey gave it time just to be sure. The seconds crawled by, turning slowly into minutes.

Confident that Kazinsky and his agents had cleared out, Kasey began to dig her way free of the garbage. Her muscles were cramping at having been confined for so long. She pushed the lid open and stood up. Stretching to her full height, she cracked her back.

"That's better." Reaching into the dumpster, she drew out the duffel. "Now to find Sanders and do something about this stench."

Kasey made her way to the mouth of the alley and paused in the shadows there. Night was falling quickly, but it wasn't yet dark. Resigning herself to the wait, she pulled up an overturned milk crate and sat in the shadow of the motel, waiting for Sanders to return.

Within minutes, the faded emerald green pickup pulled into the parking lot. Kasey snatched up her duffel bag and raced across the lot. Before Sanders could even kill the engine, Kasey had slipped into the passenger seat.

"What's going on?" Sanders asked, furrowing his brow. The scent of Kasey's current situation wafted through the vehicle. "And what on earth happened to you, you..."

"Stink to high heaven, I know. I just spent the better part of an hour hiding in the dumpster."

"The room wasn't to your liking?"

"It was, until the ADI showed up. Apparently, the clerk tipped them off. He must be one of ours."

Sanders let out a slow breath. "Glad you got out. How did you know they were coming?"

"I saw it in a vision," Kasey replied, relaxing into the seat. "I managed to clear out right as they were pulling into the building. The dumpster wouldn't have been my first choice but unfortunately it was my only option."

"Well when you put it that way, the smell isn't that bad. Thanks for sticking around to wait for me."

Kasey ran her fingers through her hair. "After all we've been through, I wasn't going to leave you to them. It was Kazinsky, after all, and I really hate that guy."

Sanders cracked a grin. "Yep, he's the worst. Don't worry, he'll get what's coming to him, but we do need to get out of here quick."

"Yep, we'll need to ditch the car tonight too, just in case, but first, I need a shower," Kasey replied.

"I'm sure it can be arranged. What's more, I think I've solved our money problem."

"Do tell," Kasey said, cocking her head.

Sanders backed up the vehicle and then tore out of the parking lot. "Soon. Let's get you cleaned up first."

# CHAPTER 2

Traveling across New York City's outer suburbs, Kasey dozed in and out of sleep. The car jostled as it eased over a speed bump. Startling awake for the umpteenth time, Kasey rubbed her weary eyes.

"Where are we?" she asked.

"Just at a local superstore. We need to get you a change of clothes. We can ditch the car here and use the gym across the road to freshen up. It should have some showers we can use."

Kasey looked at Sanders. "I may be getting pretty desperate but buying my clothes at a superstore, I'm not sure that I'm quite at that point yet."

Sanders laughed. The rich hearty chuckle was a refreshing sound after all they had been through over the past few days. They had had precious little to laugh about with the ADI breathing down their necks.

"It's just for the time being, I promise. We'll get cleaned up, get some resources, and find something a little more your style, but for the love of all that is good, we can't live on the run with you smelling like that. Either I will pass out, or you will draw the attention of everyone in Brooklyn that still has a sense of smell."

"Is it really that bad?" Kasey asked.

Sanders nodded. "Obviously you've gotten used to it. I don't know if I ever can. Let's get a change of clothes and a few snacks to tide us over. While we are at it, grab a new bag. That one is in the same boat."

Kasey and Sanders crawled out of the car. Sanders tossed the keys on the seat and closed the door.

"You're making it a little easy for the thieves, don't you think?" Kasey asked.

"That's the point," Sanders replied. "The easier, the better. The ADI will be onto the car soon enough. If someone could steal it and take it for a joyride, they would actually be doing us a favor."

Kasey had to agree. She hoisted up the duffel bag and shut the door. It wasn't much, but the pickup had managed to keep them ahead of the ADI. Kasey wasn't sure just how far she wanted to be walking while smelling like the dumpster.

She followed Sanders into the store and together, they wound their way through the aisles with a large shopping cart.

If the other shoppers thought something of Kasey's state, they kept it to themselves.

Wandering the aisles, Kasey couldn't help but throw a few snacks into the cart: a bag of chocolate and some chips. She was starving.

Sanders steered the cart toward the clothing section.

Scouring the aisle, Kasey found a pair of jeans to replace her trashed pants and a couple of T-shirts.

"You'll need something for the cold," Sanders said as he lifted a pair of hoodies off the shelf. "I'm grabbing one too."

The last time Kasey had worn a hoodie, she'd been breaking into Beth's apartment. The whole experience had gone rather poorly for her. She looked up to find Sanders staring at her.

"Come on, without it, you'll freeze. Secondly, we need to do whatever we can to conceal our appearance. So, you may find it distasteful but its privacy features will come in useful for us later."

Kasey raised her eyebrow, but Sanders wasn't elaborating.

She took the hoodie and tossed it into the cart. "Happy, now?"

Sanders cracked a wide grin. "Yes. Very much so. I know it's painful, but if we don't put in the effort, it won't be long before they pick us up. There are enough cameras in New York City they'll find us eventually. If we want to stay inside the city limits, we've got to do something to stay ahead of them."

Kasey grabbed the shopping cart. "We're not leaving. If we leave, the Shinigami get what they want. There is no way in hell I'm letting that happen. There is too much at stake."

Sanders nodded. "Don't worry, after tonight we'll have everything we need to turn the tables on him."

"Fill me in on the grand plan," Kasey said, stalling the cart.

"Not here. Too many potential eavesdroppers. I promise, I'll share soon."

Kasey stepped away from the cart.

Sanders grabbed a change of clothes for himself and started wheeling the cart toward the checkout. The clerk looked Kasey up and down, but said nothing, ringing up each of the items in turn.

"That will be ninety-three, eighty-five," the clerk said.

Sanders reached into his wallet and drew out the cash.

Kasey glanced at the wallet. With the purchase of the clothing, there was not a great deal left. They had been avoiding using debit or credit cards to avoid being traced, but their resources were severely depleted.

"Running a little low," Kasey whispered.

Sanders pulled out two fifty-dollar bills and handed them to the clerk. "Don't worry, Kasey, it won't be an issue for much longer."

The clerk jammed the notes into his cash register, drew out the change, and handed it over. After sliding the coins into his wallet, Sanders took the bags and they made their way into the parking lot.

"The pickup is still there," Kasey said, nodding at the vehicle.

"Don't worry. It won't be for long," Sanders replied.

Ignoring the vehicle, they walked through the parking lot, across the street, and into the 24-hour gym. It was getting late and Kasey hoped the attendant behind the front desk wouldn't be paying attention.

"Passes, please," the attendant asked.

*No such luck.*

"We're from out of town," Sanders said, turning to the counter. "No passes, but we were hoping we could pay for a single session."

"Interested in getting a membership?" the clerk asked, studying Kasey's disheveled state.

"No, thanks, we're only in town for the night," Sanders said.

The attendant's gaze drifted down the bags Sanders was holding.

Then, he shrugged. "That'll be twenty dollars each, thanks."

It was steep, and Kasey knew it, but the prospect of drawing extra attention was enough of a disincentive for Sanders to reach into his wallet and draw out the last fifty-dollar bill and hand it over.

The attendant snatched it and jammed it in the register before handing Sanders his change. Sanders nodded at him, then headed into the gym. Kasey followed after Sanders as they wound through the machines. She had no intention of working out.

Instead, she headed straight for the showers.

As her hand hit the door handle, Sanders tapped her on the shoulder, "Any chance you can do something with your hair color?"

Kasey paused, then ran her hand through her black hair. She loved her hair. The thought of coloring it was difficult to stomach.

She let out an exasperated sigh. "I'll see what I can do."

Sanders nodded. "Thanks, Kasey. I appreciate it."

Kasey pushed open the door to the ladies' amenities, duffel in one hand, her bag of goodies from the store in the other. Shuffling over to the showers, she stopped only to grab a towel off the shelf. Then she stepped into the shower and closed the door behind her.

Layer by layer, she peeled off each of the items of clothing the dumpster had soiled. As she pulled the T-shirt over her head, she got another whiff of her former hiding place.

"Well, I won't be sorry to see you go," she said, tossing it in the corner of the stall.

She turned on the shower and stepped under the heated jets. She let out a deep breath. The steaming water bathed her skin, driving away the stress of the day. She allowed herself a few minutes to relax, simply letting the water wash over her.

After a few minutes, she went to work purging the last vestiges of her time in the dumpster. When she finished, she stepped out of the shower and pawed around in her duffel bag for her compact. She flipped it open and narrowed her gaze into the mirror.

She was loath to cut her hair but after her time spent masquerading as Agent Helene at the ADI, she had a better idea. Running her hands through her hair, she took a deep breath.

"*Lliw Gwallt,*" she whispered. Her fingers began to glow as she moved them through her hair. Wherever they went, her lustrous black locks shifted into long blonde tresses.

Not for the first time, she was grateful for her magic. Going from such a dark tone to blonde was a feat she would have never dared with mundane hair dyes. It was the sort of job for a salon, which unfortunately was not a luxury Kasey had available right now.

The arcane dye did its job well, though. In no time, it had dyed the front portion of her hair from root to tip. Using the mirror and her compact together, Kasey slowly turned and continued administering her enchantment to ensure she managed to get all of her hair. It just wouldn't do to have a singular brown patch in a hard to reach place.

It took about ten minutes before she was satisfied that she had hit her desired tone. Raising her fingers to her face, she ran them over her eyebrows. To the extent possible, she wanted to ensure there were no obvious flaws in her disguise. She lifted the compact and moved it behind her head. Confident everything was in order, she admired herself in the mirror.

She'd never dared to go blonde. Something about it had always intimidated her. But admiring her new tresses, she couldn't help but smile.

"That's not half bad," she said to herself. Her entirely different look, combined with the change of clothes, would mean it would take more than a few glances for someone to realize it was her. Short of using an illusion to mask her identity completely, this was as close as Kasey would get.

Using magic to maintain a full body illusion was draining. Doing so for minutes was feasible, but doing it for hours or days on end was simply an untenable proposition. Kasey had no idea how the Master of Shinigami managed to do so effortlessly. The amount of energy required to impersonate Arthur Ainsley for an entire year was difficult to fathom.

Moreover, the more magical energy that she unleashed, the more likely they were to draw the ever-watchful eye of the Arcane Council. Small spells here or there might get lost in the bustle of magic that was New York City, but the amount of energy required to maintain a full-body illusion for both her and Sanders would eventually draw attention.

Kasey shut off the water and grabbed her towel. After drying herself, she dressed in her new clothes. They were a natural enough choice and would help with her disguise.

She opened the shopping bag, took out the new duffel, and loaded the few possessions she would retain into it. Then, she piled all of her old clothes and shoes into the old soiled duffel and zipped up the bag in an effort to contain the stink.

She let herself out of the stall and then deposited the entire duffel into the trash. The eighteen-year-old using the hairdryer at the sink glanced over her shoulder at the noise, but Kasey ignored her.  Shouldering her new duffel bag, Kasey made her way out of the bathroom and into the gym, hunting for Sanders. Kasey scanned the room but didn't see him.

*I'd have thought he'd beat me out.*

Turning Kasey slowly searched the room again, and did a double take. There, leaning against the wall in his hoodie and cargo pants, was Sanders. It had taken Kasey a moment to register it was him, as her fellow fugitive had done a little work himself. If she had not been hunting for him, she would have walked straight past him.

The stubble that had been growing out over the past few days of neglected shaving was now a fully-fledged beard. Instead of its usual dark brown tone, it had streaks of gray mottled through it. The salt and pepper look added ten years to his age. Not something most men would be keen to do, but clearly a price Sanders was willing to pay to keep himself out of the ADI's cross hairs.

His hair had been styled with the same attention to detail but was shorter, almost a military crew cut but it too shared the same streaky gray appearance he had affected with his beard.

Sanders was patiently scanning the gym for any sign of trouble. As she approached his gaze looked straight past Kasey. She smiled; obviously the hair was enough to fool even his heightened sense of alert.

She bounded up to him. "Hey there stranger, love the beard. Really digging the retired grandpa-slash-homeless man vibe you got going here."

Sanders did a double take.

"Wow." His gaze lingered on her hair.

"Someone has a thing for blondes," Kasey taunted.

Sanders laughed. "You know what they say, they do have so much more fun."

Kasey gave him a playful shove. "After the last few days, I'm not sure how much fun I can handle."

Sanders zipped up his hoodie. "If I'd known you'd be willing to go blonde, I might have suggested it days ago."

As they headed toward the exit, more than a few heads turned to stare at her.

"I don't know that it's having quite the effect we were looking for," Sanders whispered. "This seems to be drawing more attention than we were before."

Kasey smiled and gave her hair a superficial flick. "I know. I look fan-tas-tic."

She pretended to drink in the lingering glances of her admirers.

"Lucky me," Sanders said with a smile.

Kasey raised an eyebrow. "I don't know about that, Grandpa. Everyone here will think you're a cradle snatcher."

Sanders nodded. "That, or they will think I'm incredibly wealthy."

Kasey scoffed. "Sounds like a stretch. You're definitely looking more like a homeless person than an eccentric billionaire. You missed the mark if you were going for the Tony Stark look."

Sanders leaned in and whispered, "I am Ironman."

Kasey laughed and with the week she'd had, it felt good.

Sanders only had a couple of years on Kasey. While he hadn't made the greatest impression during their brief meeting at the Arcane Council, over the time they'd spent together the past few days, Kasey had to admit the handsome ex-director had been pretty good company. Kasey's eyes lingered over him as she followed him out of the gym.

As close as she could tell, he was single. Sanders didn't have a wedding band and hadn't made any mention of his family. Kasey had considered asking but hadn't wanted to make things awkward. Now with his appreciation of her new look, Kasey was glad she hadn't. She didn't want to give him the wrong idea.

Sanders was handsome enough and until his current predicament, he'd been a rising star in the world of magic. As one of the youngest directors the ADI had seen in over a century, he certainly had a lot going for him.

Kasey had come to appreciate his easy-going humor. In spite of all that had occurred around them, Sanders still managed to make her laugh. The last time she'd felt this way had been at the manor, with John.

As John entered her thoughts, Kasey felt a pang of guilt. She hadn't spoken to him since she had left the Administorium. Whatever had been going on between them had been put on hold by her fresh status as a fugitive. She wondered what he must be thinking. She had dozens of missed calls from him, but Kasey knew better than to use her phone. It lay at the bottom of the duffel bag, the sim card stashed in its case. She didn't want to give the ADI any opportunity to trace her movements.

*What was happening between her and John?*

It was a question she had never expected to be asking herself. Dinner had gone well enough. John had been charming and considerate, even funny at times. His help over the past few weeks had been welcome. Kasey wondered what he must be thinking. The ADI may not have known what happened at the Cathedral but they would certainly have their suspicions by now.

Regardless of how they considered that incident, Kasey breaking into the Arcane Council had put her on the hit list right next to Sanders.

John was living under the roof of the Master of the Shinigami and didn't even know it. Kasey had considered warning him, but decided against it. Telling him would only place his life in danger.

After witnessing Theo's murder, Kasey was not going to place John in harm's way like that. Unfortunately, that meant allowing him to believe she was now a fugitive aiding his father's would-be killer. She had no idea what was running through his head, and badly wanted to speak with him, but there was far too much at stake. His life, her life, and the well-being of the city depended on her taking a longer term view of the situation.

*I need to deal with the Shinigami, then hopefully he'll understand.*

"What are you thinking?" Sanders asked.

Kasey knew what she was thinking: she'd gone from no man in her life to two potential suitors, both of whom seemed interested in her, but neither of whom Kasey really understood her own feelings for.

*That is a problem for another day.* She drove the encroaching thoughts from her mind.

Turning to Sanders, she flashed a smile. "Nothing much, just wondering where we are heading."

"Oh, Kasey, just wait until you see the night I have in store for us."

"Night? You make it sound like a date." Kasey was kicking herself as soon as the words were out of her mouth.

Sanders' grin widened. "You'll never have had a date like this. Just you wait."

He raised his hand and waved down a cab. The cab pulled over, and Kasey and Sanders slid into the back seat.

"The Bronx, please," Sanders called to the driver.

The driver nodded and took off, merging into the evening traffic.

Kasey scowled at Sanders, but he only settled against the seat, smile in place.

*The Bronx. Why on Earth are we headed there?*

# CHAPTER 3

The taxi ride passed in silence, Kasey having given up on trying to pry Sanders' plan out of him before he was ready. The taxi pulled over and Kasey and Sanders climbed out of the back seat. Her feet had barely hit the sidewalk before the taxi took off down the darkened street.

"I hope that plan is going to kick in soon," Kasey said. "That was the last of my cash, and your wallet is looking pretty thin too."

"Yeah, I wouldn't worry about that too much," Sanders jammed his hands into the pockets of his hoodie. "This little stop should allow us to replenish our resources and give us what we need to strike back against the ADI."

"How do you figure that?" Kasey asked, searching in the darkness. There was nothing of note in sight. It was a run-down street in the Bronx. She couldn't see how it would help their circumstances.

"Our major problem has been running from hotel to hotel. They know we're using cash and must be running low, so they just keep moving from dingy motel to dingy motel looking for us there. There are only really so many places we could be. They are finding us through trial and error for the most part and it's only a matter of time. We can't rely on anyone we know, as they are still definitely watching them, so we are cut off and slowly running out of funds. We're about to fix all that."

Kasey cocked her head to the side. "Call me a stickler for the detail, but that still seems rather vague, and I'm not sure that I'm a fan of your choice of lodging for the night."

Sanders waved his hand, as if brushing away her concern. "Oh, relax, we won't be staying here."

"Good," Kasey replied, eying the decrepit buildings. "From what I know, gangs run most of this neighborhood."

Even with her considerable skills both as a witch and a formidable martial artist, she was in no mood to hang around.

"Just follow me," Sanders replied, "and put on your hoodie."

She dropped the duffel bag, pulled out the hoodie, and slipped into it. New York was easing slowly into winter. No doubt the coming weeks would bring with them snow. It was going to be a white Christmas.

*If there is a Christmas at all.*

With the Shinigami accelerating their plan, there was no way of knowing how much time she and Sanders had left to stop their deadly plot.

Sanders led Kasey down a dark alleyway that ran between two towering apartment buildings. Both buildings looked like they'd seen better days. One of them looked all but abandoned. A temporary fence had been erected around it, and signs announced it would be demolished shortly.

It was likely to be redeveloped in short order. Much of the Bronx was undergoing a transformation as wealthy landlords evicted their tenants and built towering new condos overlooking the city.

Kasey crept down the alley.

Sanders pulled up his hood. Reaching into his pocket, he drew out two handkerchiefs. He tied one around his face, obscuring all but his eyes, then handed the second to Kasey. "You might want to follow suit. It won't do for us to be recognized here."

Kasey took the handkerchief but raised one eyebrow. "Okay, Sanders, level with me now. What are we doing here? And why are we dressed like cheap bandits from an old eighties Western movie?"

"Well, as I mentioned before, our problem is resources. We need money, both to stay ahead of the ADI and to begin fighting back. If we are to win others to our cause, we will need to be persuasive. With the ADI hunting us, that won't come cheap. We need money, a lot of it. I figured robbing a bank was out of the question. That might impact your ability to return to your former employment. There are however many places in New York which are just as good as a bank, and this is one such place."

Kasey looked around the dark alleyway. "Where exactly are we?"

Sanders stared at the temporary fence surrounding the building. "If my sources are correct, this building on our right is one of several supply centers for the Night Crew."

"The Night Crew?" Kasey hissed. "They are one of the most brutal gangs in the city. They were responsible for more drug-related homicides last year than any other three gangs combined. They're infamous."

"Precisely," Sanders said, nodding at the building. "I spent the afternoon gathering intel to make sure we picked the right location. I knew they operated in the area, but I had to watch their couriers to track them back here. They come and go frequently. Drugs out, cash in. Even if it's not their HQ, it is certainly one of their major stash houses. There should be plenty of cash inside, more than enough for us to take care of ourselves for the foreseeable future."

Kasey shook her head, mouth agape.

Sanders' plan was audacious, but it was also suicidal. The Night Crew maintained their iron grip on The Bronx with an unwavering code of violence, bribery, and corruption. Even the NYPD gave them a wide berth.

Joint operations with the DEA had been organized repeatedly. From time to time, the NYPD succeeded in dragging some of the low-level dealers into the station, but their higher echelons of leadership had proved elusive.

The identity of their master, the Night Lord, was a closely guarded secret. His lieutenants had always been far more willing to go to prison than to snitch on him.

"You do realize what they'll do if they catch us?" Kasey asked.

Sanders nodded. "Yes. They'll kill us."

"How can you be so calm about this?" Kasey asked, raising her hands.

"Because," Sanders started, "it's exactly what the ADI is going to do when they catch us, so when you think about it, ADI or Night Crew, it doesn't really make a difference. If we don't change the game, we are as good as dead anyway."

Kasey pulled the handkerchief up under her eyes. "Yes, but with your plan, we are going to have two organizations hunting us rather than just the one we have now."

"If you have a better plan, I'm all ears. But unless we do something drastic, we're sleeping on a park bench tonight. I promise it is every bit as unpleasant as you would imagine."

Kasey had to concede the point. They were running out of options fast and she knew it. Without resources, the ADI would simply run them to ground. It might take a day, it might take a week or a month, but sooner or later the ADI would get them. There was no way of evading their attention forever, not without more resources. It was time to fight.

Steeling her nerves, she stepped closer to Sanders. "Alright, then, larceny it is. What's the grand plan?"

Sanders drew his pistol from the duffel and tucked it into the waistband of his pants before lifting the hoodie over it to conceal it. "I have one magazine, how about you?"

Kasey opened the duffel, drew out her Glock, and checked the magazine. "I've only got three rounds. Practically empty. So the plan is to take out the Bronx's most notorious criminal syndicate with less than twenty rounds?"

Sanders shook his head. "Oh, no, we would be horrendously outgunned. We'd be dead in minutes. Hardly a fair fight, if you ask me." He led the way down the darkened alleyway. "The gun is just a last resort. I wasn't planning on fighting that fair."

Kasey caught his meaning immediately. "Magic?"

Sanders nodded. "Magic, indeed. We'll be in and out before the ADI know we're on the move. By the time the ADI arrive, they will have nothing but a mess to clean up. I doubt anyone is going to believe a bunch of drug dealers when they say two wizards broke into their stash house. They will be the laughingstock of the city. It is far more likely they will simply put a price on our head and be done with it."

"Oh, is that all?" Kasey said with a wave of her hand. "I don't know what I was even worried about."

"Like I said, Kasey, if you have a better plan, I'm all ears."

Kasey shook her head. "Nope. When it comes to committing suicide, this is as good a plan as any, I suppose. Besides, willfully making a mess for the ADI to clean up sounds tremendously appealing."

"That's the spirit," Sanders replied. "The more we divide their focus, the better our chances of staying ahead of them are. Kasey, it's time to ignore all the directives you have ever been given. It's time to make as big a mess as possible."

If Sanders could see beneath her handkerchief, he would have seen her lips tighten into a broad smile. The previous days' pursuit had worn her nerves to shreds. It felt good to be on the front foot again. Doing some damage to the Night Crew appealed to her on many levels. It would take the NYPD weeks or months to build up enough of a case to get a search warrant. By that time, the Night Crew would have moved on to a new location. It was these regular relocations that had allowed them to stay a step ahead of law enforcement. It would feel good to re-balance the ledger.

Kasey cracked her fingers and began to summon her powers. "Alright, let's do this. Where are they?"

Sanders pointed down the alleyway to where it came to a dead end. A heavy steel door stood in front of them. For an abandoned building, she'd expected it to be in poor repair, but instead, this steel door had been recently installed and reinforced. It looked more like the entrance to a fortress rather than a derelict structure awaiting its end.

Kasey strode toward it, Sanders at her side.

They came to a stop.

"Ready?" Sanders whispered.

"As ready as I'll ever be," Kasey replied, raising both hands. "What's the plan?"

Sanders shrugged. "I dunno, I was just gonna knock on the front door."

Before Kasey could stop him, Sanders reached up and rapped on the heavy steel door three times.

# CHAPTER 4

A steel slider set in the door at eye height began to part. The grind of steel against steel echoed down the alley as the peephole opened. The gap was little wider than a pair of sunglasses. Through the hole, two brown eyes peered out.

"What do you want?" the sentinel asked from the other side of the door.

The alley was dark; he would be struggling to make out who was outside.

"That's easy," Sanders replied. "We want to come in. Open up."

"What's the password?" the sentinel demanded.

Kasey and Sanders looked at each other.

Sanders shrugged. "My bad, I should have expected that." He turned back to the door and in his most innocuous voice took a guess. "Please?"

"In your dreams," the sentinel replied. "Now, get out of here before I come out there and shoot you."

"I'd love to," Sanders replied. "Unfortunately, I really need to speak with your boss. Is he in?"

"He doesn't take appointments," the sentinel replied. "Piss off."

Sanders looked at Kasey. "What you'll notice is that wasn't a no." Addressing the thug he pressed on. "Come on, surely he'll make an exception for some old friends. Go get him."

"I said get lost," the sentinel shouted, slamming his fist against the door to scare them off.

Kasey knew what was coming next.

The sentinel shoved the barrel of an ugly black revolver through the peephole. "Now, get lost."

Kasey grabbed the steely black barrel of the revolver and pushed it down so that it faced nothing but the empty alley.

The thug grunted as he pulled the trigger. The pistol bucked as the gunshot reverberated through the alley. The bullet struck the pavement, sending flecks of concrete spraying from the impact.

The barrel rotated as the firing pin drew back once more.

Before the sentinel could pull the trigger a second time, Sanders slammed his palm against the outside of the fortified door and bellowed, "*Bernstan Stiele.*"

The steel door buckled, its hinges exploding in a shriek of twisted metal. The door sailed inward, like it had been struck by a battering ram, taking the sentinel with it.

Sanders stepped through the opening. Bending over the sentinel, who was pinned beneath the door, he said, "Sorry, chief, mine is bigger."

Kasey kicked away the sentinel's pistol.

"That's going to hurt in the morning," she muttered, nodding toward him.

Sanders shrugged. "He should have opened the door when I said please. "

Kasey found herself standing in a hall. Its carpet was a dull green weave that was worn and fraying at the edges. The décor may have seen better days, but it seemed the Night Crew cared little for interior design. Their efforts focused instead on security, such as the fifty-caliber machine gun emplacement dominating the far end of the hallway. The weapon was fortified with sandbags to shield it from anyone who might storm the building.

Someone seeking to rob the Night Crew would have to walk straight into the business end of the heavy machine gun. Unfortunately, right now, that included Kasey.

Beside the machine gun nest rested a table at which sat three Night Crewmen playing cards. Kasey's heart skipped a beat as one of them leapt into the emplacement and popped up behind the machine gun.

"Sanders!" Kasey warned.

Sanders looked up the hall at the thugs.

Kasey glanced around for a way out. Spotting an apartment door to her right, she hurried over to it. Just as the machine gun racked its payload, she kicked in the door.

Grabbing Sanders, she tackled him out of the hall and into the apartment, pinning him to the floor. Milliseconds later, the machine gun opened fire, shredding the hall in a storm of steel.

Fortunately, the placement of the weapon didn't allow for great angling of the weapon. That didn't stop the guards from trying.

The emplacement fired, its withering salvo pounding the rooms to smithereens. On the floor, she and Sanders were beneath the worst of it. She cringed at the racket and she continued to hold Sanders down.

The hallway went still as the machine gun's feed ran dry.

Sanders tapped Kasey on the arm. "Let's go, before they reload."

"With pleasure." She rolled off him.

Getting to her feet, she made for the doorway. She raised her right hand before her.

"*Pêl Tân!*" She chanted as she rounded the shattered door jam and re-entered the hall. Channeling her will, she sent a coalescing ball of flames hurtling toward the machine gun emplacement.

The thugs' eyes went wide as the flames sailed toward them. Kasey strode down the hall, the fireball billowing before her. She was an avatar of destruction.

The blaze rolled over the sandbags, engulfing the thug who was still trying to reload the machine gun. The thug collapsed, shrieking in pain.

His comrades at the table lifted their weapons.

Kasey cocked her head to one side. "Wrong choice, boys."

Chanting, she sent the inferno into overdrive. The flames blossomed outward, catching both thugs in its frenzied expansion. The fire consumed the thugs along with the wooden table they had been sitting at.

With a flick of her wrist, she extinguished the blaze.

Sanders nodded his approval. "No half measures."

"Nope, they would have killed us if we'd given them another chance."

She had little compassion for the fallen Night Crew, unlike the ADI agents they had been evading for the past few days. The ADI agents were innocently following orders and weren't aware of who was giving them. The Night Crew were willfully profiting from a life of crime. Their fortune was built on the misery of those they enslaved with their drugs.

As she looked up, she caught a flicker of movement out of the corner of her eye. She ducked, and the thug's blow sailed over her head. He caught Sanders in the face. Sanders staggered back into the hall.

The thug grabbed Kasey by the hoodie and wrenched her off her feet. She took advantage of the closing distance and slammed her fist into the man's nose.

The thug grunted at the blow but didn't release her. Instead, he slammed her into the floor. She grunted as the wind was driven from her lungs. Fighting the throbbing pain in her back, she swept the legs out from underneath the thug.

He came thundering to the floor as Kasey rolled out of the way. Leveraging herself against the wall, she bounced to her feet once more.

The thug drew his pistol.

*I'm not close enough to reach him.*

Kasey stared down the barrel of the pistol as the thug's finger tightened on the trigger.

Movement shifted beside him. Sanders brought a chair down on the thug's arm. The pistol went off, sending a round into the floor. Dropping the pistol, the thug grabbed the chair and shoved it and Sanders out of the way.

Kasey spotted the pistol laying in the hall. The thug's gaze settled on it too. Kasey dove on the weapon, snatching it off the ground. As she raised the gun, the thug's hands closed around hers. She tried to turn it on the thug, but he was using his weight to keep the weapon pinned against the ground.

*If I can't use the weapon, I need to take it out of action.*

Kasey squeezed the trigger, discharging the pistol into the floor, over and over, until the pistol simply clicked. It was empty. She dropped the weapon so that her hands were free.

Before she could react, the thug wrapped his arms around her throat and began crushing it with his bulging biceps.

Kasey tried to mouth the words to a spell, but it died in her throat. She couldn't get a word out. Her head was going light from the lack of oxygen.

With the last of her strength, she hoisted her feet side up to the wall, and pushed off it with everything she had.

She grimaced at the impact as her head struck his already broken nose.

He released her. Kasey gasped for breath.

His hands went to his ruined face as blood ran from his nose.

Unable to use her magic for lack of breath, Kasey grabbed the pistol from the ground. Changing her grip, she brought it around and pistol whipped him across his head.

The man collapsed, rolling back on to the floor unconscious.

Brushing herself off Kasey found Sanders behind her, catching his breath

"Thanks for your help. The next one's yours," Kasey muttered.

"Fair enough," Sanders replied. "That one hit like a freight train."

Above them, an alarm blared to life.

Kasey looked up. "Well, safe to say they know we are here."

"Indeed. Nothing changes, though. We need to keep moving," Sanders replied. "The quicker the better."

Footsteps raced around above them as the building came to life.

"There goes our element of surprise," Sanders laughed.

"It was gone the moment you blew in the door," Kasey muttered. "Not that it matters. Let's get a move on. We need to get that money and get out of here before any reinforcements arrive."

"What reinforcements?" Sanders asked.

"Other chapters of the Night Crew. If this place is as important as you think, we are going to have every Night Crewman in the Bronx on their way here now. So, we need to be out of here before their friends arrive."

Sanders nodded. "So, I guess that just leaves one question. Do we take the elevator, or the stairs?"

# CHAPTER 5

Kasey took the stairs two at a time as she raced to the second floor. As she cleared the landing, she came face-to-face with a tall mountain of a man.

The thug before her looked Eastern European and had a thick mop of brown hair reaching down to his shoulders that did little to cover a distinct scar that ran from his right eye down to his ear. He looked like he'd gone toe to toe with someone with a broken bottle and lost badly.

Whoever it was must've had balls of steel or been very drunk. The thug was easily seven feet tall and as wide as Kasey and Sanders put together.

"There's a problem downstairs." Kasey started. The bluff was unconvincing, and she knew it.

Without a word, the thug snapped out his arm and grabbed her. The cheap material of the hoodie tore as she was hoisted into the air.

She kicked wildly, catching him in the groin. The ogre grunted in pain but kept a firm grip on her.

"Are you kidding me?" Kasey said, clutching the thug's arms. "That almost always works."

She kicked again, but this time the thug was ready. He simply held her farther away, her legs flailing helplessly in the air.

Sanders' footsteps bounded up the stairs after her. He came to a halt at the entrance, right behind her.

The thug hefted Kasey and threw her straight at Sanders. Sanders tried to duck, but she slammed into him. They tumbled backwards and thudded down a flight of stairs. They collapsed in a heap on the landing.

Kasey groaned as she fought to extricate herself from Sanders.

Sanders struggled to his feet. "Rest assured, that was no more pleasant for me than it was for you." Motioning at the stairs, he continued. "Care to try again?"

Kasey struggled to catch her breath. "Oh no, this one's all yours."

The thug started down the stairs toward them.

"Have at him," Kasey said with a nod.

Sanders looked up as the thug closed in with a wild haymaker. Ducking under the blow, Sanders drove his fist straight into the man's solar plexus. The thug groaned but gave no other acknowledgment of the hit. Instead, he launched another punch at Sanders.

Sanders sidestepped the blow. The thug stumbled forward, sailing between Kasey and Sanders, and punched the wall. His meaty fist shattered straight through the plasterboard. Without hesitating, he yanked his hand free of the wall and turned on Kasey once more.

"Enough!" Kasey shouted, stepping in. She drove her fist straight into the man's kidneys. She launched a second and a third, landing all three punches in quick succession.

The thug swung his right arm to backhand Kasey as he turned.

Ducking under the blow, Kasey puffed as she threw another punch at his chest. As her fist closed the distance between them, Kasey closed her eyes and channeled her energy. Lacing the blow with arcane energy, she chanted *"Haearn!"*

Her fist hit the towering thug like a freight train. His eyes bulged as his chest caved beneath the thunderous blow. The momentum of her magic threw him back into the wall he'd just drawn his fist out of.

The plasterboard put up little resistance. The thug landed between two beams, wedged into the wall cavity. He barely resisted as he struggled to gain his breath. Kasey suspected that she may have punctured a lung.

Sanders drew back and delivered a thunderous blow to the thug's chin. The thug collapsed; his weight carried by what was left of the wall as he slumped unconscious.

"He's going to hate life when he wakes up," Sanders said, staring at the thug.

"Serves him right for tossing me down the stairs," Kasey replied. "And look at this, I just got these clothes today and already they're trashed."

She pointed to a large hole in the front of her hoodie. The material had torn when the thug had dangled her like a rag doll.

"Well, let's hope there's just the one of those, shall we?" Sanders asked. "Because I hate to think of what might have happened if he'd connected with one of those punches."

Kasey brushed back her hair. "Let's hope we never find out."

Together, they started back up the stairs. This time, Kasey took them one at a time, her eyes scanning for threats ahead.

As they reached the top of the landing, angry shouts carried down the hall. The language was foreign to her, but the tone was readily understandable. They were furious.

Kasey peered into the hallway. Like the first floor, apartments lined either side. Since they did not know the layout of the Night Crew's lair, they would have to sweep the building room by room to find what they sought.

Kasey held her finger to her lips. She listened for the direction of the shouting. She and Sanders crept down the hall to investigate. As they moved, they opened doors, checking each room. The small apartments were completely empty, the tenants having been evicted months ago.

At the end of the hall, they found the last door closed. From within the closed apartment, the shouting continued unabated.

Sanders held up his fingers and slowly counted down with them, one, two, three. Reaching three, he kicked in the door.

The lock broke, and the door swung inward. In front of them sat two tables in what had once been a lounge room. Piled high on each table were packages wrapped in silver foil stacked neatly in tight formations like bricks on a pallet. Each of the tables was stacked almost as tall as Kasey. Standing behind the table were three thugs. One of them was shouting orders while the other two busily tried to load the bricks onto a trolley.

At the commotion, the thugs whirled about.

Sanders advanced on the three thugs. They were shorter than their compatriot on the stairs, but they were heavily armed. The man barking orders drew a silver pistol from his waistband

and pointed it at Kasey. The two brutes loading their trolley abandoned their labors and reached for the AK-47s that were draped across their backs.

*I'll never reach them in time.*

Sanders called to Kasey, "You shield us, I've got them."

Kasey nodded and began to chant, hastily drawing a shield around them. The translucent barrier washed over them until it completely enveloped them in its protective embrace.

It shimmered to life right as the thugs unleashed hell. The automatic rifles spat fire and death in a devastating fusillade. The bullets struck Kasey's barrier and ricocheted wildly around the room. The noise was deafening as the leader added his own weight of fire to the fray. The shining silver Desert Eagle bucked as he discharged each shot.

Despite the chaos, Sanders' focus was second to none. Kasey could not hear his words, but she watched his lips move. The rightmost thug's jaw dropped open as his weapon began to wheel around of its own accord. The thug strained against the weapon as he fought the invisible force of Sanders' magic, but the assault rifle continued to fire as it emptied the last of its magazine straight into his companion.

The leader looked momentarily surprised, as if the man had been a traitor, then turned and shot him at point blank range.

He released the magazine on his weapon, dropping it to the floor, and drew a second in the same deft motion. The magazine slammed home and the man was firing again before Kasey and Sanders had the luxury of taking advantage of the situation.

Safe behind Kasey's shield, Sanders chanted once more. The Desert Eagle began to glow. It was subtle at first, as if the weapon was reflecting the overhead light, but soon it turned an angry shade of red. The leader flung it to the floor and shook his hand. His palms were scorched red at their brief contact with the burning weapon.

He turned to run, but there was nowhere to go. Kasey and Sanders, in their shield, blocked the doorway. Behind him, the second-floor window had a significant drop beneath it. It wouldn't kill him, but it would injure him. Before he could make the decision, Sanders closed the distance and drew his own weapon, pistol whipping the thug with extreme prejudice. The man collapsed in a heap.

"Is that what I think it is?" Kasey asked.

"Cocaine," Sanders replied. "A lot of it, too. That much must be worth millions."

Kasey sighed. "This isn't quite what I was expecting. I was hoping for cash."

She nodded at the table laden with drugs.

"Me too," Sanders said. "It has to be somewhere though. With this much product, we've clearly found one of their stash houses. If the drugs are here, so is the money. It must be upstairs."

Kasey followed Sanders to the door but paused. Looking over her shoulder, she called to Sanders. "We can't leave all this here. If this reaches the street, it will destroy thousands of lives and fund their activity for months to come."

"There will always be more drugs. It's like trying to stop a tidal wave with just your hand."

"Yeah, but these drugs can still destroy lives now." Turning, she put out her arms and focused on the mountain of narcotics. "*Pêl Tân.*"

Flames erupted from her outstretched hands before hurtling into the tables. Focusing her mind, she increased the intensity of the blaze.

In a matter of moments, tens of millions of dollars' worth of narcotics disappeared in the fire storm, leaving only a scorched mountain of ashes.

Kasey cracked a grin. "That ought to help put a dint in the Night Crew's business."

Sanders pointed to the door.

Kasey hurried toward him and gestured. "After you, Sanders. Age before beauty."

"Ladies first, I insist," Sanders replied.

Kasey shrugged and strode back into the hall.

The sound of weapons being racked filled her ears.

She halted, looking up.

"Oh, my word," Kasey muttered as her heart stopped.

# CHAPTER 6

At the far end of the hall stood a wall of Night Crew wielding assault rifles. Kasey only had one avenue of escape open to her. She drove straight back into the room where the Night Crew had been storing their narcotics. As she hit the floor with Sanders, gunfire erupted from the end of the hall.

Hundreds of rounds filled the narrow hallway, turning it into a death trap. If not for her quick thinking, Kasey would have been riddled with bullets.

After a withering round of fire, the Night Crew halted.

"Holy hell," Sanders began. "These guys are packing more firepower than a small army."

"Well, from what I've heard at the Ninth Precinct, most of their hardware is purchased from black-market suppliers overseas. They are certainly the most heavily armed of the gangs currently plaguing New York. On the rare instances that the NYPD do go after them, we normally require a complete SWAT deployment. Our patrols simply end up outgunned. A few months back, one of the units from the Eighth Precinct stumbled onto a Night Crew warehouse. Not realizing what they had found until it was too late, both them and their squad car were cut to ribbons. The Night Crew have no respect for law enforcement. They are far more afraid of their overlords than they are of anything we can do to them," Kasey said from where she remained on the floor.

"Well," Sanders replied, "I'm not with the police and they ought to be terrified about what I can do to them."

He picked himself up off the ground and approached the door.

A steady advance of footsteps moved toward them. Kasey went to get up, but Sanders motioned for her not to move. At the door, he simply drew his weapon, reached around the door jamb, and emptied the magazine down the hall.

There were shrieks as Sanders' shots slammed into the Night Crew. Several bodies struck the floor. With the solid mass of Night Crew moving toward them it would have been impossible to miss. In spite of their losses, the Night Crew pressed on, their advancing footsteps still audible against the wooden floorboards of the hall.

Sanders dropped his spent weapon and raced away from the door. In mere milliseconds, the entire door frame was riddled by automatic weapons fire.

The Night Crew alternated between advancing and firing cover fire at the door of the room Kasey and Sanders were now huddled in.

"They aren't going to give you another chance to do that," Kasey replied.

"Nope," Sanders shouted between gunshots. "They are going to wish they had, though, because I'm a lot less dangerous with a gun than I am the other weapons I have at my disposal."

"Magic?" Kasey asked.

"You better believe it," Sanders replied. "I just wanted to bait them in, so we don't have to chase them down.

The thugs were getting closer and closer every minute.

Kasey and Sanders got to their feet.

"We can't go out that way," Kasey replied. "There is too much firepower. Tanking that many bullets earlier was more draining than I would have liked."

"You're right." Sanders looked from the door to the apartment wall. "What we really need to do is flank them, and I think I have an idea."

While the Night Crew pushed up the hallway, Sanders approached the wall that divided the stash room from the apartment next door. Reaching the wall, he raised his hands and muttered an incantation. His voice was faint, and Kasey could barely hear him.

Before her eyes, the section of the plasterboard wall, already pockmarked with gunfire and bullet holes, became translucent.

As Sanders continued to chant, a section of the wall appeared to vanish entirely.

He gestured toward her. "Come on, Kasey, through here quickly."

Kasey followed Sanders through the portal-like opening and into the next room. He closed his fist and the portal dispersed. Kasey found herself looking at the solid, albeit beat up, wall once more.

"That was new," Kasey whispered. "You're going to have to teach me that one. Did we just walk through a solid wall?"

"Yes and no," Sanders replied with a grin. "That particular spell shifts the constituent atoms apart until there is nothing but empty space. Technically, we walked through nothing, but the effect is much the same."

"They didn't teach us that at the Academy," Kasey replied.

"No, I imagine not," Sanders answered looking around the new room. "Can you imagine the mischief students would get up to if they could walk through solid walls? As far as I know, I am one of the first to have attempted that particular spell. It's a blend of magic and science. I've never even seen anyone else try it."

"You mean you invented it?" Kasey asked, raising an eyebrow.

"Not quite. I read about a wizard who was able to do it in an old case file but like many ancient spells, it's something that has been forgotten or fallen into disuse over time. Perhaps because of the complexity of the enchantment. If you get it wrong, the wall can re-materialize with you still inside, and the results would be highly undesirable."

"I see," Kasey responded, biting her lip. "Still, that could come in handy. You'll have to teach me later."

Sanders smiled. "I can do that. Keep in mind though that I spent weeks practicing that one in the archives, before I was game to try it in the field. Probably best not to attempt it while we have gun wielding maniacs closing in on us."

Sanders raised his hands and approached the next wall. "Here we go, in ancient English, the word you want is *Naht*. I am not sure of its Welsh equivalent. The key is to ensure your mind is clear. Your only thought should be the wall before you and your desire for it to be made up of nothing but empty space. You only want to move the particles for a moment, you don't want to move the wall entirely. For them to return, I would chant *Edcierr*."

Sanders mouthed the incantation once more and the wall before him moved. In moments, there was simply a shimmering portal into the adjacent room.

"Love it," Kasey replied, charging into the next room.

Sanders continued guiding them through room after room until they had slipped past the advancing Night Crew in the hallway.

When they reached the final apartment, Kasey headed for the door and cracked it open. She peered out. The Night Crewmen at the far end of the hall were readying to breach the room she and Sanders had been in only minutes before.

Their attention was wholly occupied by the room they are about to storm. Kasey risked a glance to the left toward the stairs. There was no one there. Pulling the door open, she stepped into the hall, Sanders right behind her.

The Night Crew raised their weapons and rushed into the stash room. Silence fell over the floor. A moment later, the Night Crew filtered back into the hallway, muttering amongst themselves. They stopped and turned their attention to Kasey and Sanders waiting for them.

Kasey and Sanders bellowed their incantations in a glorious duet of deadly magic. Lightning leapt from Kasey's outstretched palms, arcing down the hallway at the speed of light. Sanders unleashed a volley of arcane missiles. Together, their spells turned the hallway into a war zone.

The Night Crew didn't have a chance to raise their weapons before the arcane fusillade tore through them. Kasey's lightning collided with their front rank, sending thousands of volts through their unprotected frames. Lightning surged through their bodies before earthing itself into the hallway floor. As the first row of men collapsed, Sanders' barrage sailed over them and struck those behind them.

The Night Crew might have been the most fearsome gang in all of New York City, but they had never had to face a magical onslaught and their weapons were no match for the energy employed against them. Their faces were drawn, their jaws open in slack-jawed terror.

Those who had been shot by Sanders earlier had got off light.

Kasey may have had compassion for the innocent, but for those who profited from the misery of millions, she had none. She continued hurling arcane energy down the hallway.

A hand on her shoulder dragged her back to the present.

"Pretty sure that's all of them, Kasey," Sanders replied. "Let's keep moving. Only one more floor to go. The money must be up there. That's where these guards came from."

Kasey sucked in a deep breath to calm herself. Following Sanders, she made for the stairs. Together, they took the final staircase. Kasey searched ahead as she went.

They rounded onto the landing. To their surprise, the top floor of the apartment building had also already been partially demolished and somewhat remodeled. Instead of a hallway with apartments running off it, they found the entire floor was now a single open plan space. The only exception was a large steel room that dominated the back right-hand corner. Around the room laid a series of weapons cases that had been opened.

In the center of the room was a large wooden desk and seated behind it was a Caucasian man in his forties. The man's sandy blond hair was dappled with the first hints of gray. Wrinkles at the corner of his eyes spoke of terrible stress as did his creased forehead. The man appeared to be unarmed.

Kasey and Sanders approached him cautiously.

"I take it you two are responsible for the destruction below?" the man asked, his voice surprisingly neutral.

"Indeed, we are. Your men resisted and were dispatched as a result. You ought to learn from their mistake," Sanders warned.

The man raised both hands in submission. "Pray, tell, what brings you to the Night Crew's territory? You have to know that an attack such as this is suicidal. You may have killed a few foot soldiers, but we number in the thousands. We have a veritable army behind us."

"For all the good these ones did you," Kasey replied, pointing to the floor beneath.

The Night Crewman smiled. It was unsettling.

"Are you the Night Lord?" Sanders asked.

The man chuckled. "Heavens, no. I'm merely a Lieutenant. So, if you've come for him, you are going to be bitterly disappointed. Who are you, anyway? Assassins? Rival gang members? Feds?"

"None of the above," Sanders replied. "I'm going to need you to open that safe though."

The man laughed, hitting his palm against the table. "Not on your life, my friend. The alarm has already been raised. Reinforcements will be here in moments. You may as well leave while you still have a chance. Rest assured I will not be opening the safe. It would be worth more than my life to do so."

"It will cost you your life if you don't," Kasey said. "So be about it quickly."

"Very well," the man replied. "I'll need my key card." He lowered his hands and reached under the desk. Kasey looked to Sanders, but he had already made up his mind.

As the lieutenant raised his pistol, Sanders bellowed his incantation. *"Beadumaegen!"*

The spell hit the Lieutenant full force. The desk flipped and threw the lieutenant with so much energy that he sailed straight through the glass window behind him.

The lieutenant screamed all the way down, his terrified shrieks ending abruptly a few short seconds later.

"Why do they never learn?" Sanders asked.

"Well, I'm sure if he knew what magic was, he might have reconsidered his decision," Kasey replied. "But he had no way of knowing what was coming next. To him we looked unarmed."

"Be that as it may, he died in vain. We hardly need him to open the safe." Sanders approached the steel structure. "I think we have found what we are looking for."

Kasey nodded. "You have to admire their preparation. This is some serious hardware for a safe house."

"Indeed, with guns and drugs in these volumes, their cash-flow must be insane."

"We're about to find out," Kasey said. "Do you want to do the honors, or shall I?"

Sanders looked at the safe. "Steel is a lot more draining than plasterboard to attempt to pass through, I think I might just carve this one open."

Approaching the vault, he raised his hands and began chanting. A thin beam of red energy leapt out from his outstretched palm and struck the vault. Where the lance hit the safe, the steel glowed red.

Kasey looked at Sanders. Sweat ran down his brow as he continued his assault. She could feel the heat radiating from the safe even from a distance, but Sanders continued undeterred.

Under the searing heat, the steel wall began to liquefy. Great sloughs of molten steel ran free and slumped to the floor as Sanders moved the focus of his spell in an ever-increasing circle. He continued until the chamber beyond became visible through the expanding rend in the safe's wall.

In less than a minute, there was a hole in the wall large enough for them to pass through. Sanders closed his fist, ending his enchantment.

Kasey stepped forward but Sanders put his arm out. "Just give it a moment to cool. If you touch one of those molten flecks, it will be a world of pain. That's several thousand degrees of heat right there. It will melt straight through your boots."

Kasey swept a hand before her. "*Gwynt Oer.*"

A blast of super chilled vapor washed from her outstretched hand, bathing the devastated wall. The molten steel hissed as the vapor struck it.

In a matter of moments, Kasey dropped the temperature in the room to almost freezing. The vault hissed in angry protest as the superheated steel was snap frozen by the plunging temperature.

Kasey shivered as she started toward the hole.

"Don't mind if I do," she called, ducking into the vault.

As the mist cleared, Kasey stopped.

The vault had to be at least 30 feet long and 20 feet wide. Lining the vault was row upon row of pallets. Each of the pallets contained a mountain of cash. The notes had been neatly stacked, bound, and then shrink-wrapped to keep their shape.

Kasey let out a low long whistle. Sanders was only a step behind her.

He surveyed the vault and then shook his head. "That must be almost one hundred million dollars. If they aren't hundreds, it may be a little less. Blows your mind to see how profitable a life of crime is, doesn't it?"

"It didn't work out for these guys," Kasey replied.

"True," Sanders replied. "But, whoever the Night Lord is, with this much cash, his reach must be enormous."

"Yup, we better get a move on. Reinforcements will be here any minute. I doubt our friend the Lieutenant was bluffing. We need to get as much of it as we can carry and get out of here."

Sanders picked up a box cutter from on top of a nearby pallet and attacked the shrink wrap. Then, he placed his duffel on top of the stack and began loading it with cash.

Kasey followed suit, ignoring the stacks of tens and ones in favor of the fifties and hundreds. It took less than two minutes for her to completely fill her bag. As she slung the duffel back over her shoulder, she realized it was a lot heavier now and would certainly impede her movement.

"I can't say that I've ever carried enough cash to be weighed down by it," Kasey stated.

"It's a first for me too," Sanders replied. "It may weigh a ton, but we're going to need it. As for the rest of it, I don't think we should leave anything for the Night Crew, do you?"

He headed out of the vault and stopped just outside of it.

Kasey followed him through the hole. Straightening up, she cracked a smile. "I agree. Besides, I've never had cash to burn." She focused her energy on the pallets laden with cash and shouted, "*Pêl Tân.*"

Her spell set the pallets alight. She and Sanders stood side by side, transfixed as they watched tens of millions of dollars go up in flames.

After a moment, Kasey said, "I have to be honest. I can't help but think of all the good it could have done."

Sanders nodded. "It's true, but we were never getting that much out of here before reinforcements showed up."

The sound of screeching tires drew their attention outside. Kasey ran to the window that the Lieutenant had abruptly exited through minutes earlier and looked down.

More than a dozen black SUVs had pulled up outside.

"What is it, Kasey? Sanders asked.

"Reinforcements." Kasey replied, shaking her head. "Lots of them."

# CHAPTER 7

Kasey looked down through the shattered window, taking in the army of Night Crew that was converging on the battered stash house. A dozen vehicles had pulled up in front of the abandoned apartment complex. She could also make out members of the Night Crew picketed along the street. Doubtless there would be others that she couldn't see.

Sanders approached the window and studied the street below.

"I was hoping it would have taken them a little longer to respond," Kasey said.

"Yes, it seems this particular stash house was nearer and dearer to their heart than we might have hoped. With the mountain of cash that was in there, it's hardly a surprise." Sanders patted his duffel bag.

"Any ideas on how we can get out of this?" Kasey asked.

"The same way we got into it," Sanders said. "One level at a time."

As the Night Crew filed out of the vehicles, they began arming themselves with an assortment of semiautomatic weapons, submachine guns, and even a handful of assault rifles.

The Night Crew was ready to do battle.

Kasey searched the stash house's inner sanctum and spotted the weapons crates that still lay open.

"We need to thin the herd," Kasey called, racing to the nearest crate. "If we use their weapons until they get closer, they'll have no idea what to expect. Let's hold our magic in reserve, just in case."

Sanders nodded and rushed over to the weapons cache. He reached into the black polymer crate and drew out an AR-15 assault rifle and three magazines. After jamming one magazine into his rifle, he shoved the other two into his pockets for later.

Kasey had other ideas. Her crate contained MP5 submachine guns. She'd seen them in action at the Met Gala and knew they were brutally efficient. Drawing one, she prepped it and racked it, ready for action. She was about to leave when a crate beside her caught her eye.

"That will do nicely," Kasey whispered to herself. She reached into the crate, and began shoving the MK II fragmentation grenades into her pockets before hurrying back to the window.

"What are you doing?" Sanders called out.

"Slowing them down," Kasey replied as she studied below.

The Night Crew was preparing to breach the first floor. Kasey lifted the grenades. Pulling the pin on two of them, she tossed them at the street below, one at a time. Before they had hit the sidewalk, she sent another pair sailing through the broken window.

She watched the grenades bounce off the sidewalk. The Night Crewman nearest one of the grenades shouted a warning, but it was too late. The grenade detonated mere feet from the gathering thugs. The blasts filled the air with lethal shards, obliterating the thugs. Their shrill screams filled the night air.

A second blast detonated as the third and fourth grenades bounced under the nearest SUVs. The results were deafening. Night Crewmen went down like wheat before the scythe, while the grenades that landed under the nearest SUV detonated with spectacular style. The SUV had largely shielded the Night Crew behind it until the car itself exploded, adding its own deadly shrapnel to the mix.

Sanders raised the AR-15 to his shoulder. With Sanders' elevated position, the Night Crew below were horrendously exposed. With clinical efficiency, Sanders went to work emptying the first of his magazines in disciplined bursts.

He dispatched dozens of members of the Night Crew before ducking back inside the window. He pulled Kasey down next to him. Seconds later, the entire window, along with the roof of the room, was bracketed with automatic weapons fire.

Sanders hunkered down, unable to lend any more fire to the fray without presenting an easy target in the window. The element of surprise had been lost.

"Into the building. Get inside now!" an angry voice shouted from below. In spite of the terrible toll that had been wreaked on their number, the Night Crew were unperturbed.

The wail of their wounded comrades filled the air, but the Night Crew paid them no heed. They were far more intent on storming the building.

"We need to get out of here, Kasey," Sanders replied. "The longer we stay, the worse it is going to get. You heard the Lieutenant—they have no shortage of manpower. What we need to do is get past them as quickly and efficiently as possible."

Kasey nodded. "The sooner we get out here, the better."

Remaining low, they scrambled, with their duffel bags, out of the room. Once in the hallway, they straightened and darted for the stairs. As they bounded down them, voices rose from below.

Down they ran, closing the distance to the ground floor as quickly as they could. They had almost reached the second-floor landing when they were met with voices on the stairs directly beneath them.

The Night Crew sweeping the building were making swifter progress than Kasey had hoped.

As rapid footsteps drew nearer, Kasey raised her weapon. Two Night Crewmen rounded the corner, racing up the stairs toward them.

In their haste, they ran right into the waiting mouth of Kasey's MP5. Gritting her teeth, Kasey squeezed the trigger. Both of them slumped to the ground as the submachine gun cut them down.

Furious shouting rose from the floor beneath. "They are on the stairs, take them out."

Kasey and Sanders turned and ducked into the second floor. A brutal fusillade smashed into the stairs right behind them.

"There is no getting out that way," Sanders replied. "The bottom floor is overrun. We're going to need another exit, or a distraction."

As Kasey considered their quandary, more Night Crew appeared on the stairs. Sanders dispatched the Night Crewmen with a short burst.

The Night Crewman fell, but not before he dropped a round object onto the landing.

"Grenade!" Sanders shouted.

As the grenade skittered across the floor, Kasey shouted an incantation: "*Gwthio!*"

Her spell caught the grenade and drove it back toward the stairs. The grenade slipped back through the banister and dropped to the floor beneath. There was a deafening explosion as the frag grenade unleashed its lethal payload among the advancing Night Crew.

"That was close," Sanders replied, panting. "Way too close. We need to move."

"Well, we can't go down there. Not yet, there are way too many of them," Kasey answered.

"Then we go back up," Sanders said. "We use the building and spread them as thin as possible. When they split up to search the building, we try to break through their ranks."

Kasey and Sanders raced back up the stairs.

The Night Crewmen approached more cautiously now. Periodically, Sanders would lean over the balustrade and fire his assault rifle down the staircase. Each time, the Night Crew would halt and unleash a withering salvo of return fire.

Twice more as they retreated upstairs, Kasey and Sanders picked off the advance scouts of the Night Crew who had grown overconfident.

Reaching the fourth floor, Kasey racked her brain. Soon they would be pinned down in much the same manner as the Lieutenant had been. There was plenty of firepower in cases on the fourth floor, but they would eventually be overrun.

Beneath them, the advance of the Night Crew echoed through the building. Floor by floor, they swept with single-minded purpose. If Sanders and Kasey had hid in one of the rooms below, the Night Crew would already have rooted them out.

As the Night Crew moved steadily upward, Kasey seized on the one avenue they had yet to try.

"Sanders," she called, "the elevator."

"It's suicide," Sanders replied. "The second the doors open, we're going to be cut to shreds."

"Exactly," Kasey replied. "That's why we're not going to be in it."

Kasey mashed the button for the waiting elevator. Its aluminum doors parted and Sanders reluctantly followed her inside. Slinging the strap of her MP5 over her shoulder, Kasey pushed the elevator's service hatch. The hatch popped open, revealing a pitch-black cavernous space above.

Sanders caught on quickly. Intertwining his hands, he boosted Kasey into the space above the elevator, then pressed the button for the ground floor.

As the lift descended, Sanders handed his AR-15 to Kasey. She pulled it up, then reached down for him. He took her outstretched hand, and she helped hoist him up through the hatch and onto the roof of the elevator.

She had expected the elevator to be stopped in its descent as soon as the Night Crew discovered it on the move. Angry shouts filled the air as they rocketed downward, but the journey from the fourth to the first floor was swift.

With an eerie chime the elevator doors opened. As they parted, the elevator was rocked by a merciless burst of weapons fire. Bullets shredded the aluminum walls like paper as the Night Crew unleashed their anger.

Kasey waited on top of the elevator, next to Sanders. She could barely breathe.

"It's empty," A thug shouted. "It's just a distraction. Radio upstairs and let them know to keep searching. They're up there somewhere, and we need to find them and kill them, or the boss will have all our heads."

As the thugs returned to their search, Kasey lifted the elevator hatch and peered down through the gap. Several Night Crew congregated before the elevator. She reached into her pocket and drew out the last of the frag grenade that she had looted from the weapons cache upstairs.

She pulled the pin and hurled it through the open hatch.

The grenade skittered along the floor into the waiting Night Crew.

"Grenade!" someone shouted, but it was too late. The grenade detonated with terminal intensity in the confined space of the hallway. The waiting Night Crew were annihilated.

Kasey dropped down through the open hatch and whipped her MP5 up to her shoulder.

Sanders dropped down behind her, AR-15 at the ready.

The hallway, however, had been decimated. More than a dozen bodies were scattered down its length, some from Kasey's most recent grenade, others from the earlier gunfight at the staircase. The Night Crew had fared poorly.

"Let's go," Sanders called, leading the way down the hallway, rifle at the ready.

"Not that door," Kasey replied. "There are others waiting out front. Let's head out the back, the same way we came in."

"They could just as well be waiting for us there too," Sanders replied.

Kasey slid a fresh magazine into her MP5. "I have no doubt they will but there is going to be less of them, and we won't be nearly as exposed. We'll only have to watch the alley ahead and the door behind us. We'll have fewer surprises that way."

Kasey led the way toward the alley. Above them, the Night Crew milled about in confusion. She and Sanders made it to the back door without encountering any other resistance. At the door, she hurriedly slipped out into the alley. Sanders followed right behind her.

She froze.

Up ahead, two vehicles sat across the mouth of the alleyway. Behind them, half a dozen Night Crew waited, their weapons raised and ready, pointed directly at her.

The Night Crew opened fire. Kasey dove behind a nearby dumpster, dragging Sanders with her. The steel vessel took the worst of the fire. Bullets ricocheted wildly around the confined alley.

"Kasey, we can't stay here," Sanders hissed. "We'll be killed."

"I know. We're going to have to clear that alleyway."

"I need a second to catch my breath," Sanders panted. "Do you think you can shield us for a few moments while I gather my strength?"

Crouching behind the dumpster, Kasey was less than enthusiastic, but there was no way out except through the blockade.

"I can, but I won't be able to hold them for long," she said.

Sanders sucked in a deep breath. He was fit but clearly not as fit as Kasey. Sweat ran down his brow as he rested against the brick wall.

Kasey focused her mind and summoned her shield. *"Tarian!"*

A shimmering red shield materialized around them.

If the gangsters were confused by the glowing red shield growing behind the dumpster, it didn't show. They simply continued pumping firepower down the alley in a bid to destroy their elusive targets.

With each moment, Kasey felt her energy waning. The longer she had to maintain the spell and the greater the weight of fire the more quickly she would tire.

"Whatever you are going to do, do it quickly," Kasey whispered.

When Sanders didn't respond, Kasey looked over her shoulder. He had lowered himself to a runner's pose and was beginning to glow. Kasey stared in wonder as he glowed brighter and brighter.

"When I say now, expand your shield as wide as you can. I only need a little bit of cover. Once I get moving, the bullets won't matter anymore."

Kasey had an inkling of what was coming. She'd seen that golden glow once before, at the Ainsley's Manor.

"Now!" Sanders shouted.

Kasey closed her eyes and willed her barrier outward, stretching its protective shield as far as she could manage. She couldn't see it, but she heard Sanders take off. Her eyes fluttered open, and she risked a peek around the dumpster to see Sanders sprinting down the alleyway toward the cars. Soon the light grew in intensity until Sanders was completely obscured by a radiant glowing orb of energy.

Kasey knew what came next. She shrank back behind the dumpster and drew her shield tight around her.

With singular purpose, Sanders' spell reached its cataclysmic finale.

Kasey felt the shockwave roll over her. Debris rained down from the buildings above.

As the dust settled, she dared another glance down the alley. Sanders stood there smiling in the midst of the Night Crew barricade... Only the barricade was no longer there. Both vehicles had been flipped by the blast and lay in the center of the street. The thugs were nowhere to be seen.

Sanders' glow was fading with each second. Kasey pushed to her feet and raced to meet him, duffel bag pounding against her back. As she emerged from the head of the alley, the battered bodies of the Night Crew came into view. They weren't moving at all.

Without a word, she and Sanders sprinted down the street and around the corner. The storefronts were closed, heavy steel grills blocking all of the store entrances, and the street was largely deserted. Sanders grabbed Kasey and pulled her into the entryway of a butcher store lying just ahead of them.

"What are you doing?" Kasey asked.

Sanders chanted, "*Bedydrian.*"

Before her eyes, Sanders' countenance shifted, and in seconds, he'd aged his entire appearance once more. He now looked like an octogenarian reaching the end of his life.

Hunching over with a cane, he cracked a toothy grin. "You're next."

Before Kasey could stop him, he cast the enchantment. Kasey's heart stopped as her arms wrinkled and sagged as the illusion rolled over her.

Even in the dark, she resembled a woman three times her age. She was also carrying a grocery bag, rather than the black duffel.

"I'm going to kill you," Kasey muttered.

"Not now you aren't," Sanders replied, hefting his own grocery bag off the sidewalk.

They stepped out from the storefront right as two Night Crew happened upon them.

"You there. Stop!"

Kasey and Sanders stopped dead.

Sanders feigned surprise and turning slowly, raising his cane.

"What is it?" His voice came out weak and strained.

The Night Crew approached, taking in their appearance. Their faces contorted with confusion.

"I, um…" the first Night Crewmen muttered.

"What is it?" Kasey added, trying her best to affect an old woman's nag.

"Have you seen anyone else pass this way?" the second Night Crew asked. "We were looking for some thieves. They were dressed in black hoodies."

Sanders pointed his cane toward an alley trailing off the right-hand side of the street. "We saw two people run down there, just a moment ago. I'm not sure if they are your thieves but they certainly looked like they were up to no good."

The two Night Crew took off towards the alley.

As soon as they were gone, Kasey grinned. Maybe this disguise wasn't so bad.

Tottering to the edge of the street, Sanders held up his cane and hailed a taxi.

In moments, one of New York's signature yellow cabs pulled over. Sanders motioned for Kasey to jump into the back seat. She ducked inside, scanning the distance for any sign of more Night Crew.

The taxi driver clambered out of his car.

"Shall I put that in the trunk?" He nodded towards the grocery bags.

Sanders clutched the bag close. "No need, son. They can ride with us in the back."

The taxi driver shrugged and then climbed back into the vehicle. Sanders lifted the bags into the back of the cab and slid them across the seat before climbing in after them.

"Where to?" the taxi driver asked

"The Park Hyatt, please," Sanders said, settling against the seat.

The taxi pulled out into the street.

"They certainly looked like they were up to no good," Kasey teased affecting her best impression of Sanders' old man accent.

"Quiet, you. It was the best I could do on short notice."

Kasey couldn't help but laugh. "What's the plan now?"

Sanders patted the shopping bags with their precious payload.

"Tonight, we rest." He turned his gaze out the window, watching the street. "Tomorrow, we strike back."

# CHAPTER 8

Raiding the Night Crew stash house, while risky in the extreme, had provided them with all the funds they needed to lose their pursuers, at least for a time.

Now with their cash reserves replenished, they were no longer slumming it. At Sanders' insistence they had headed for the Park Hyatt located near Central Park. The ritzy hotel would throw the ADI off their tail, at least for now. The five-star establishment cost more than a thousand dollars a night and offered spectacular views of the surrounding city. It was the perfect place to relax and catch their breath while they formulated the next stage of their plan.

Checking in under assumed identities, and masked by an illusion spell, Kasey was confident they could breathe easily at last. The ADI may have been looking for her and Sanders, but Ben and Jenny Kaswell were fine and upstanding citizens with money to burn.

Safely ensconced in their suite, they had counted their haul. Avoiding the smaller denominations had paid off. Together, the two duffel bags contained almost three million dollars. Packed flat and banded together in neat ten thousand dollar stacks, it was remarkably compact.

Kasey had never seen so much cash in her life.

Off the grid and armed with resources, they now had a swathe of options available to them. Eyeing the luxurious hotel beds, Kasey succumbed to her exhaustion.

Flopping onto the mattress, she drifted straight to sleep.

The sound of the hotel door clicking shut roused Kasey from her slumber.

Kasey fought to open her eyes.

"Good morning, sleepyhead," Sanders said from nearby.

Kasey forced her eyes open to see Sanders sitting at the writing desk in the suite. The lights were dimmed, and a tray with a large silver lid rested on a serving cart by the bed.

"I wasn't sure what you wanted, so I got you a little bit of everything. I figured you'd be famished."

Kasey sat up, eying the tray hungrily. "Mmm. Breakfast would really hit the spot about now."

Sanders smiled. "At this time of day, it's more brunch, really."

Kasey brushed her hair back out of her face. "Really? What time is it?"

She searched the hotel room.

"It's almost eleven am," Sanders said. "Fortunately, these black out curtains work like a charm."

He held up a remote and pressed one of its small black buttons. The heavy curtains rolled back, revealing a bright and sunny New York day. Kasey squinted against the sunlight, but as her eyes adjusted, she took in the spectacular vista that was New York City. Central Park cut a trail of green through the urban metropolis as it stretched for miles below her.

"I've certainly stayed in worse places," Kasey said, "I'm pretty sure most of them were your fault though, so this makes things even."

"I don't know about that," Sanders replied, "I was a wizard in good standing before you walked into my office. I'm beginning to think my run of ill fortune can all be traced back to a singular source."

"Oh, get out of here," Kasey replied, rolling her eyes. "You were wanted for murder before I got involved. You did that much all on your own. As far as I can tell, your success in evading your fate has more than a little to do with my intervention. If it wasn't for me, you'd be in a cell—or worse."

"Worse, definitely worse," Sanders said, turning all the way around to face her. "And I've certainly had poorer company that's for sure."

Kasey glanced down at her sheets to avoid the compliment, but found the warmth rising in her cheeks regardless. She rubbed her face then reached for the cart.

"What have we got here?" she asked, changing the subject.

"Enough  to feed an army," Sanders replied with a flourish of his hand.

Kasey lifted the lid off the tray. To her delight, Sanders wasn't exaggerating. It was the largest tray she had ever seen. On one plate lay crispy bacon and scrambled eggs. On another two, toasted waffles heaped with whipped cream and chocolate sauce. Beside them, rounding out the meal, were two slices of French toast on a wooden board, drizzled in maple syrup. This close to Canada, and in a hotel of this caliber, Kasey expected it would be sensational.

Kasey giddily picked up her knife and fork and set to work. After slicing a portion off the first waffle, she picked it up and slid it between her lips, savoring the moment.

Between mouthfuls, Kasey turned to Sanders, "So what's next? We are no longer poor as church mice, but the ADI will catch our trail eventually. We still need to change the game."

"I have a few ideas," Sanders replied, folding his hands over his stomach. "I've been thinking on it for most of the morning, but I've only come up with one truly viable course of action. If we want to get the ADI off our back, and do away with this baseless murder charge, we need to prove my innocence. Right now, the Master of The Shinigami is masquerading as Arthur Ainsley. As the chancellor, the complete resources of the Arcane Council are behind him. He killed Theo to cover his tracks and we are still paying the price for it. Our freedom hinges on taking him down."

"I agree, but that's far easier said than done." Kasey swiped her finger through the whipped cream and dabbed it on her tongue. "How are you suggesting we accomplish so great a feat? Arresting him will be difficult. All the money in the world is still going to make that a tricky proposition. Besides, he's a formidable wizard. The more we pursue him, the more perilous our own position becomes. Not to mention the collateral damage that might result from such an effort. He's not going to go quietly."

"I agree entirely," Sanders said, leaning forward. "Arresting him will be nigh on impossible. We have no evidence of his crime. It's our word against his."

"The council will not take our side." Kasey answered. "Of that much I am sure."

"Agreed. So I think it's time we commit the crime for which I already stand accused. I'm suggesting we kill Arthur Ainsley, or at least the impostor who has taken his place. It will be far easier for us to eliminate him than arrest him."

Kasey nodded slowly. She had always known it might come to this. The Master of the Shinigami was the author of a plot that would kill millions. He had to be put down for good, but hearing Sanders suggest killing him while he sat in power at the heart of the Arcane Council seemed almost tantamount to suicide.

"You want to assassinate the chancellor of the Arcane Council?" Kasey asked.

Sanders leaned back in his chair. "No, he's already dead. I want to kill the pretender now sitting in his place. It will take care of two birds with one stone. If we kill him, the illusion he's hiding behind will be shattered, revealing his duplicity and prove his motive for killing Theo Getz. It will clear us of all suspicion and allow us to take back control of the Arcane Council. Hopefully with him dead, the plot against the city will also fail."

"Two birds with one stone, indeed," Kasey said as she slowly chewed a piece of crispy bacon. She swallowed it before continuing. "But it's a heck of a big stone." She studied Sanders expression. "How do you suggest we accomplish that?"

"I'm still working on the details," Sanders answered, "but we now have resources we didn't have yesterday. Money buys allies, equipment, and weapons. I'm suggesting we use this money to pay for it. I'm suggesting we buy ourselves an army of our own."

"An army? I like the sound of that," Kasey said, mulling over the words. "Any chance I can relax here in the hotel while they take care of things? Maybe have a spa day or a massage?"

"Not a chance," Sanders replied. "Right now, there are very few people I trust in this world. I need your help to finish this. No one knows as much about the Shinigami as you do, and your visions have saved my skin more than once already. I need you with me."

Kasey let out an exaggerated sigh. "Very well, then. Can I at least finish my breakfast? Carrying out an assassination on an empty stomach is not a proposition I can agree to."

That broke Sanders' somber mood, and he laughed. "Of course. Finish your breakfast, then we'll get moving."

Kasey tore into the balance of her meal, taking a brief break now and then to gulp down her orange juice.

Sanders flicked on the TV. The usual news cycle had been replaced by a red warning screen.

Side by side pictures of Kasey and Sanders dominated the TV. White letters on a black background read, "New York's Most Wanted."

The voice over announced, "Noah Sanders, age thirty-five, and Kasey Chase, age twenty-eight, are wanted for a violent armed robbery committed in the Bronx last night. Heavily armed, the pair stormed an apartment building, terrorizing the aging residents before stealing anything they could carry away from the scene.

"No less than twelve people were killed in this brazen theft, making it the single deadliest armed robbery in New York in recent years. Authorities warn that the pair remain at large and are to be considered armed and extremely dangerous. If spotted, do not attempt to approach them. Please call the FBI's hotline on 1-800-225-5324 with any tips or sightings. A reward is being offered for any information leading to the apprehension of these two violent killers."

Kasey's jaw dropped. "What the hell?"

"The ADI," Sanders answered. "This is their retaliation for the attack on the stash house. The amount of magic we used against the Night Crew will have drawn their ire. We left enough witnesses for them to be mopping up after us for weeks. We've divided their resources, and this is how they respond. They've turned the entire city against us."

"It isn't true, though," Kasey replied, thumping the mattress. "Is there no end to the lies the ADI will tell to achieve their mission? My family will have seen that. My boss, Chief West at the Ninth Precinct, will have seen it. They've just ruined my life!"

She hurled her cutlery across the suite and leapt to her feet, hot with rage.

"Easy, Kasey," Sanders replied, but kept his distance. "This is what they want. They want to rattle us. Force us to make a mistake. This is what they do. They don't care what the cost is. They will protect the World of Magic at any price and right now they see us as the biggest threat it has faced in decades. If we want them off our back, we have to take out the Shinigami."

"That's going to be difficult with all of New York City after us," Kasey replied. "We won't be able to take ten steps before someone spots us."

"You're right. We'll have to use our aliases everywhere we go. A bit of hair dye isn't going to cut it. We'll need to use full body illusions. Don't worry about your job, Kasey. The Ninth Precinct will do its research and discover, if they don't already know, that it was a Night Crew stash house that was hit. All the damage the ADI does to us, we can undo later. For now, we just need to focus and move forward with our plan."

Kasey simmered with rage as she paced the floor angrily.

*I'm no murderer.*

She'd dropped bodies, certainly, but no one who didn't have it coming. Danilo had been the first. The finality of it had shook her then but she'd reconciled herself to the knowledge that it had been Danilo or her. She had been fighting for her life.

The Shinigami likewise didn't cause her to lose any sleep. For New York to be saved, there was a price to pay. More would be required to thwart them, that much she was sure.

The Night Crew had been the first Kasey had actively sought out. They were not self-defense. Self-preservation perhaps, but not self-defense. It had bothered her less than she had expected. She'd seen enough bodies in the morgue to know the price their drug trade was taking on the city. The victims got younger and younger as dealers pushed products laced with deadly chemicals. College students were dying in the war on drugs and the single greatest contributor to that loss of life was the Night Crew. Truth be told, when Kasey considered the lives she'd taken raiding their stash house, she felt entirely justified. She wasn't losing any sleep over their loss, either.

She stopped and stared at the full-length mirror hanging on the wall.

*What have I become?*

"Penny for your thoughts?" Sanders asked. "You're looking a little grim."

"I was just thinking about the past few months. Only months ago, I'd never killed anyone. I'm not even sure how many people I must have killed last night. The grenades alone must have taken a dozen. All told, it could have been as many as thirty people. I tell myself they were drug dealers making millions off others' misfortune, but what does that make me?"

"It makes you a hero, Kasey," Sanders said softly. "Without you, many more would have died. Danilo, the thieves at the Gala, the Shinigami, and even the Night Crew. If you'd not intervened, the loss of life would have been considerably more. We may have been motivated by survival rather than the greater good last night, but the fact remains, we just dealt the single largest blow to the Night Crew that has been struck since they took up residence here in New York City. That makes you a hero. Don't ever forget it."

"So the end justifies the means?" Kasey asked, not looking at him.

"In this case, yes," Sanders replied. "It's not a time for half measures. Think about what will happen if we are caught. Who will remain to stop the Shinigami's plot? The ADI? No, they will be dancing like puppets on a string, unaware of the usurper in their midst. The police? I'd like to hope so, but even your friends are helplessly outgunned by the Shinigami's arcane might. If we do not survive to thwart their plan, everyone you know and love in this city will die. I shouldn't need to tell you. You've seen it."

Kasey hesitated. She'd witnessed it dozens of times over the years. There was no doubt of the widespread devastation the city would face.

Finally, she said in a low voice, "Yes."

"Then steel yourself, Kasey, because there is every chance the worst is still to come."

# CHAPTER 9

Kasey followed Sanders into the bar. The room itself was unremarkable; only a few patrons sat at the counter, draining their sorrow. Sanders ignored them and headed past a set of pool tables to where a row of dingy jukeboxes and photo booths lined the back wall.

Sanders parted the curtain on the photo booth and motioned for Kasey to get in.

Pressing a hidden button beneath the photo booth's dash caused the wall to open, revealing a bar that had seen better days.

The decor seemed almost willfully run down. Perhaps to ensure that any who stumbled across it, didn't bother to remain. Those frequenting the bar looked like they belonged in the police line up at the Ninth Precinct.

Kasey suspected most of them had done time, be it Rikers or elsewhere. Where exactly the Arcane Council locked its troublemakers up was a question she'd yet to find the answer to.

Sanders guided her through the pub to a hallway which ran past a series of restrooms and a stockroom. Without reference to anyone, Sanders simply pushed open the door to the stockroom and wandered in. Stacked behind a row of kegs and liquor was an unmarked flight of stairs that simply plunged down into the darkness.

Kasey followed Sanders down the stairs.

Trusting in Sanders, Kasey made the descent. After what seemed like several stories and more stairs than she cared to count, dim LED lights flickered along the ceiling, providing faint illumination as they continued downward.

Deep beneath the city Kasey and Sanders made their way down the seemingly endless set of concrete stairs. With each flight, the raucous din from below grew in intensity. Exuberant cheering filled her ears as they descended deeper and deeper beneath the city.

"What is this place?" Kasey asked, shouting over the din.

When Sanders didn't respond, Kasey grabbed him by the shoulder and shook him.

Sanders turned. "What?"

"Where are we going?" Kasey asked again.

"A gathering place of sorts. Somewhere the seedier element of New York City is happy to congregate. Believe it or not, there are plenty of people who prefer to live their life on the out with the Council and the ADI. Most of them pass through here."

"If so many of them are all in one place, why doesn't the Council take them out?" Kasey asked.

Sanders laughed. "For much the same reason that the Night Crew still exist, I suppose. Large numbers and a predisposition toward violence. For the Council to try and regulate this place, it would require they expend lives to try and bring it under control. It would be open war. Not a healthy proposition for anyone."

Kasey nodded. It made sense. Often, law enforcement had to take a similar view when the resources to end a particular issue outweighed the upside for doing so. Sometimes, the potential costs were too high, as was definitely the case with the Night Crew. Wiping out their scourge would doubtless cost the lives of dozens, perhaps even hundreds, of officers. It was a price the city wasn't willing to pay at the present time.

"I'm told there are other entrances to the underground, but this is the only one I know of. I suspect that there are tunnels and bolt holes scattered all over the city. Another reason the Council doesn't bother. By the time we win control of it, the most wanted criminals would likely have gone to ground, anyway."

Kasey nodded, following Sanders into the bowels of the Earth. In the dim light, she examined his disguise. Today, he looked like an army veteran. At a glance and without knowing any better,

Kasey would have pegged him to be in his late forties, rapidly approaching his fifties. His hair was styled into a short crew cut. He wore a simple T-shirt and khaki pants.

Kasey's illusion was a touch on the younger side. To others, she would seem a woman in her later thirties. She'd retained much of her trim figure. Her dirty blonde hair was pulled back into a single sporty ponytail. Her wardrobe consisted of some athletic wear and sneakers.

They had the appearance of a couple out for an evening jog, but their plans this evening were more ambitious. The disguises served two purposes. First, it would allow them to travel the streets undetected. The routine changing of their identities ensured the ADI remained oblivious to their presence. Looking for them now would be like tracking an invisible needle in a mountainous haystack.

The second reason for the disguise was Sanders' position in the magical community. As the former head of the ADI, it would not serve them for anyone in the underground to recognize him. Between those who would want his head and those who would want to turn him in for the reward, there would be a lineup of those wishing to take a shot at them.

Their current identities marked them as Ben and Jenny Kaswell.

Sanders had suggested that traveling as a couple might help throw them off the scent. Kasey agreed. She would take any edge they could get right now.

Not for the first time, she found herself thinking of Sanders.

*His name is Noah.*

When she had first met him at the Arcane Council, his omnipotent attitude and outright dismissal of her story had enraged her, but as she had gotten to know him better, she'd found that her earlier impressions were wide of the mark.

He truly was a gifted wizard, well-studied and creative in his use of his arcane powers. His unfailing desire to serve the greater good even when it threatened to imprison or execute him was something she could admire. Most would become jaded by their own organization turning on them. Sanders was simply galvanized and determined to make a difference. He would clear his name and protect the Council, even if it killed him.

Every time Kasey thought she had her bearings, her life was turned upside down. At least this time, some good had come from it. In the last two weeks, her biggest detractor on the council had become her greatest ally.

*And my husband.* Kasey found the corners of her mouth creasing up into a smile at the thought. *He's not hard on the eyes, either.*

"What are you smiling at?" Sanders asked.

Kasey snapped out of her momentary daydream and caught Sanders' gaze. "Nothing. It's just nice to be out of the hotel."

"Sure is," Sanders replied as they continued downward.

Kasey thought of John, who she hadn't spoken to in days. The last she'd seen him, she had told him that his father was going to be murdered in the cathedral at St Patrick's. It would be difficult to explain to John why she had been spotted breaking into the ADI with Sanders. John might very well think she had turned against him and his father. After all, John had no idea his father was already dead, and that the man with whom he was currently reconciling was none other than the Master of the Shinigami.

The Master had stolen his father's place almost a year ago. Kasey had wanted to tell John, but it was too dangerous. Any misstep might see John dead, just like Theo Getz. The stakes were just too high to risk it.

As Kasey thought of John and Noah, she felt conflicted.

*Men, they complicate everything.*

To her relief, the next step leveled out onto a concrete landing. The landing opened into an immense concrete tunnel.

Kasey crept forward, Sanders next to her. Reaching the end of the dark passage, they found a steel door set in a concrete wall. It looked like a nuclear bunker taken out of a Hollywood movie. Before the door stood two burly bouncers in leather jackets that struggled to contain their impressive forms.

The first settled his gaze on Kasey. "What do you want?"

"What everyone wants," Sanders replied, holding up a roll of cash he'd brought from their supply. "We want to have some fun."

The bouncer nodded and held out his hand.

Sanders peeled two hundreds off the wad and gave one to each of the bouncers. "Two Benjamins for the two of us."

The bouncer eyed the notes hungrily and took them. After pocketing the note, he pulled open the heavy vault-like door.

The door swung open as the noise inside reached a crescendo.

The crowd was chanting wildly.

"Dozer, Dozer, Dozer."

It was deafening. Kasey passed through the door and found herself in an immense underground cavern. Ten feet in front of them, the concrete ended abruptly, a crude steel rail preventing anyone from falling over the edge. Kasey approached the rail.

Her eyes widened at the spectacle that greeted her. The vast underground opened beneath her. The piece of concrete she stood on was actually something of a balcony. Two more tiered balconies stretched out beneath them.

At the center of it all stood a large steel cage. Razor wire was coiled around it, leaving an empty space ten to fifteen paces wide. The no-man's land separated the dense mass of people from the action in the steel cage.

The entire underground was packed with spectators cheering at the commotion inside the cage. Bookies hustled through the crowd taking bets on the outcome, but as Kasey studied the cage below, she realized the outcome had already been decided.

Dozer was easily identifiable. The stocky barrel-chested thug with biceps the size of Boston stood in the center of the ring. His over-muscled torso seemed to blend seamlessly with his head, giving the illusion that the man had no neck whatsoever. Dozer's opponent, a Caucasian man in his thirties, was well over six feet and probably a good six inches taller than his brawny foe. He was well-muscled himself but paled next to Dozer.

It seemed he had made the fatal mistake of letting Dozer get within his reach. Now, he was being held aloft over Dozer's shoulders as some kind of bizarre trophy.

"Dozer, Dozer, Dozer," the crowd cheered.

Drinking in their adulation, Dozer did a lap around the cage, his prize still firmly clutched in his grasp. As the crowd reached the zenith of its excitement, Dozer hoisted him up into the air like a barbell and hurled him into the steel cage.

The fighter collapsed in a crumpled heap, battered and broken. At this distance, Kasey couldn't clearly make out the extent of his injuries, but the man wasn't moving.

She had seen enough to know he wasn't getting back up. He would be lucky if he lived at all. The crowd went wild as Dozer threw both hands in the air.

Bookies paid out winnings and shrugged off the bitter complaints of those whose money had been taken as Dozer steamrolled their champion.

Sanders pointed below, and Kasey followed his meaning.

*More stairs.* Kasey sighed.

Together, they wound their way down the internal staircase. On the ground floor, they shouldered through the masses as they worked their way across the underground. Sanders guided them to a cordoned off cavern that had been carved into the wall.

Red ropes dangled between silver bollards, marked the edge of the arena and beginning of what appeared to be a nightclub. While the bollards might have been ineffectual against the seething masses, the four enormous bouncers guarding the entrance certainly provided a second deterrent. Having just witnessed the brutal bout in the arena, Kasey had little doubt what might happen to someone foolish enough to enter the cavern unbidden.

Regardless, Sanders moved toward it. Clearing his throat, he approached the bouncers.

The first bouncer raised his hand, his palm facing out. "You there. What are you doing? Hell is closed to the public this evening."

"No worries. I'm not after the bar," Sanders replied. "I'm here to see the boss."

The burly security guard raised an eyebrow. "The boss?"

"You heard me," Sanders said. "I want to see Hades, now."

The bodyguard stepped away, heading down a hall at the back of the club. He left his three companions to keep an eye on Kasey and Sanders.

Kasey studied the security guards. Leaning over to Sanders, she whispered, "They don't appear to be armed."

Sanders eyed their muscled forms. "Yeah, no need for guns here. They're probably wizards, just like us. The underground isn't open to normals."

Kasey nodded. This was more magical beings than she'd seen in one place since leaving the Academy.

The head security guard re-emerged. "The boss will see you now, but be warned, Hades doesn't like being interrupted, and he hates time wasters even more. This better be important."

"It is," Sanders replied.

The security allowed them past, and Kasey and Sanders entered the private club. The only person inside the otherwise empty bar was a handsome bartender in his twenties with a large mohawk. The room had several booths and a hallway leading into the back that disappeared deeper underground.

Flanked by two of the security guards, Kasey and Sanders made their way through Hell, heading for the back of the club. Here in the hallway, the stark concrete was replaced with more elegant furnishings. The carpet was plush and black, and gold-embossed wood panel walls lined each side of the passage. They passed a row of portraits, each depicting a champion standing over his foe in the ring. At the end of the hall they came to a stop before an immense set of double doors. The doors had large glass panels that were heavily tinted.

Security opened the doors, revealing Hades' private office.

The elaborate room was dominated by a large mahogany desk. An eighty-inch flat screen sat on one wall with several recliners set out like a movie theater before it. A wall of filing cabinets ran along one side. Above them a rack of weapons held several automatic rifles. A pair of doors led deeper into the underground complex.

Behind the table, a man sat in a high-backed leather chair, with a woman sitting on his lap. His deep olive complexion complimented his brown eyes. A thick mop of black hair had been cut just above his shoulders. He wore a set of slacks with an open collared dress shirt and suspenders. Tucked under each arm was a holster. At this angle, she couldn't make out exactly what type of pistols they were, but Hades was not making any effort to conceal the weapons.

The woman in his lap wore a set of tight leather pants that threatened to burst at her every movement. The low-cut tank top left little to the imagination. Her black hair was short and styled into spikes pointing every which way. In her hands she held a bowl of grapes.

Kasey caught her gaze, and the woman snarled at her.

*Delightful.*

Hades looked Kasey and Sanders up and down as they entered, and then pointed to the chairs in front of his table. They took the offered seats.

"So, what do we have here?" Hades said. "Two supplicants come to the gates of hell to speak with Hades himself. What is it you want?"

*Oh, boy, what an ego.*

Kasey bit off her smart remark as shadows loomed over her. Their escorts had taken up position behind them.

"I have come to talk business," Sanders said. "You control the underworld, Hades, literally and figuratively, and we find ourselves in need of some muscle. "

Hades eyes continued to rove over them, drinking in every detail of their illusion.

"Well, you might want to start with who you are. I don't do business with strangers," Hades replied, leaning forward to accept a grape from the woman resting on his lap.

"Sure, I'm Ben and this is Jenny. We've recently found ourselves on the receiving end of some unnecessary oversight and would like to be rid of our oppressor."

Hades nodded. "I take it you're referring to the Council."

"Indeed, I am," Sanders said shifting in his seat. "In particular, a certain member of it. He's using the Council's resources to retaliate against us, and we'd like to resolve the situation."

Hades eyes narrowed on Sanders. "Peacefully?"

Sanders shook his head. "Permanently."

"So, you want to take out a contract against a member of the Arcane Council. That's no small feat. Sure, we have agents willing to take on that kind of work, but they won't incur the Council's ire for pocket change. We're talking six figures, may be even half a million, depending who it is you are after."

Sanders leaned back in his chair. "What's the price for Arthur Ainsley's head?"

Hades rocked forward as he burst into laughter, threatening to unsettle his companion, who remarkably managed to retain her position on his lap.

"Arthur Ainsley, the Chancellor. You must be mad. The man is currently being guarded by most of the ADI. Rotating details, hidden tails. He's guarded night and day. It's a suicide mission."

"I don't know about that," Sanders replied. "We've been watching him. His detail grows lax and lazy, too long on high alert. They are starting to grow weary. Tell me, Hades, are you seriously declining my proposition or are you merely haggling on the price?"

Hades smiled. "I like you, Ben. You've got big brass balls, but we have a problem." He leaned forward, all the levity gone from his expression. "The problem, Ben, is that I don't know you. You've walked in here unannounced and want me to embark on some insane errand against the Chancellor of the Arcane Council. No one is here to vouch for you. If I didn't know better, I would say this is some kind of ploy to draw me out and get me arrested."

He waved his hand, and fabric rustled against fabric.

Weapons were being drawn. Kasey glanced at the mirror mounted along the wall and realized that the escorts had both drawn their weapons. The barrel of their pistols rested mere inches behind hers and Sanders' heads.

*I guess they're armed, after all.*

Kasey shifted a little, angling herself just the faintest bit to try and position herself to take the man behind her.

Sanders slowly reached across and placed his hand on hers, warning her not to move.

He looked at Hades. "You may not know us, but that's something we can fix. This doesn't need to end poorly, Hades. We have offered you a potentially lucrative business proposition that also facilitates you removing your greatest nemesis. If the only obstacle between you accepting it is getting to know each other a little better, why don't we break open a bottle and fix that problem right now?"

Hades' eyes narrowed on Sanders. "That's not how it works around here. We don't know you. If you want to do business in the underworld, and more particularly, if you want to do business with me, the only way we are going to trust you is if you put your money where your mouth is. If you have the stones to step into the cage, then we have a deal."

Kasey gripped the arms of her chair. They were caught between a rock and a hard place. Even if they could overpower the two men who had them dead to rights, they still had Hades in front of them and who knew how many other security personnel waiting in the rooms beyond. Besides, they needed Hades help.

Fighting their way out wasn't going to help, so Kasey suppressed her instincts and remained in the chair.

Sanders nodded. "Very well. I accept your terms, I'll get into the ring, and you'll handle my contract."

Kasey whipped around to face him. He was a competent wizard, but he was no brawler. It would be a bloodbath.

Hade's mouth creased up into a grin. "Excellent. I was just wondering who would step into the arena next. We've had a shortage of challengers lately. Dozer is going to be thrilled."

Sanders shrank visibly. He had to go toe to toe with the maniac that had just mauled another man in front of their eyes.

Kasey was beginning to regret the foray into the underworld.

Hades' companion let out a sneer.

"Not him, my dear," she said. "Dozer has just eaten his dinner, so why not give him some dessert?" She pointed at Kasey. "Put her in the cage. Let's throw princess to the lion and see what happens."

Kasey met her gaze. Her angry brown eyes bored back into Kasey's soul.

She had seen that look before. Her eyes were full of murder.

# CHAPTER 10

Worried creases formed above Sanders' brow. She could understand his feelings. She was not thrilled about the prospect of stepping into the cage with the gargantuan brute.

Sanders rose to his feet. "You can name your price, but you can't pick which of us is to pay it. I'll not have you throwing my wife to the wolves just to satisfy your pet's petty jealousy."

Hades' guard placed his hands on Sanders' shoulders and forced him back into his seat.

"I will do as I please. Remember, if you die down here, no one will ever find your body," Hades replied. "You talk a big game, going after the Arcane Counselor. I'm yet to be convinced you aren't one of his stooges. The cage separates the wheat from the chaff."

Kasey watched as Sanders struggled against the man's hands on his shoulders. Things were deteriorating quickly. She had no idea what she had done to earn the ire of Hades' pet, but it mattered little. The only way forward was into the cage.

"I'll do it," Kasey muttered. "If you insist on this charade, I'll do it, but you better keep your word. If I make it out of that cage and you renege on our agreement, I will come for you." She clenched her fists.

"Your wife has spirit, Ben, I'll give her that." Hades laughed. "I'll make you a deal, Jen. You make it out of the pit at all, I'll give you a discount. You don't even have to win, you just have to keep your pulse." He extended his hand. "Do we have an accord?"

Kasey rose to her feet and clasped his hand. "We do. Let's get on with it."

Hades' pet giggled with giddy delight. "Dozer's going to have fun with you."

"Like you wouldn't believe," Kasey replied.

Hades stood and headed for the door. "If you are in such a hurry, let's get on with it. I imagine the crowd is growing restless with the wait, anyway."

Flanked by the escorts, Sanders and Kasey left the office. Hades led the way out of the office and through the club. As he stepped out of Hell and into the underworld arena, the crowd parted around him.

Hades touched his hand to his throat and muttered an incantation. Kasey couldn't quite make out the words over the din but the otherworldly glow at his fingertips was difficult to ignore.

"Ladies and gentlemen, denizens of the underworld. It is I, Hades. For your viewing pleasure, I have prepared a treat. Two guests have meandered into our midst, seeking a deal with the Devil."

The crowd roared its approval.

Hades raised his hand for silence. "But we won't treat with any old pedestrian who makes their way into our den. To prove their worth, they will enter the cage."

"Dozer, Dozer, Dozer," the crowd chanted.

Hades wound his way through the tangle of razor wire and up the steel steps to the door of the cage. Reaching out, he clasped the spindle wheel affixed to the gate. As he turned the wheel, two pieces of steel retracted, unlocking the gate. The steel bars popped free, and the gate swung open.

Hades gestured at the open portal. "Come now. You don't want to keep Dozer waiting."

Sanders followed Kasey through the wire to the cage. Dozer waited, flexing eagerly for the raucous crowd.

"You don't have to do this. We can find another way," he whispered.

"No, there's no going back now. We have too much at stake. If we have to go through that brute to get it done, so be it."

"Don't let him get his hands on you, Kasey. He'll break you in half."

"He will try," Kasey whispered. "I'll see he lives to regret it."

She stepped into the cage, and the gate clicked shut. The heavy grinding of steel against steel told her the spindle wheel had locked into place.

She was trapped. Kasey looked to Sanders, who stood by the cage, his brow furrowed with concern.

Hades descended the stairs. As the crowd stared in silent anticipation, Kasey watched Hades approach Sanders.

"I have to admire her spirit," Hades said. "I hope there is something left of it when Dozer is done with her."

Sanders jammed his sweaty palms into his pockets. "I'm more concerned about your man, Dozer. My wife has been known to lose her temper on occasion."

"Princess?" Hades asked. "Please, she doesn't stand a chance. Dozer is the finest brawler we have ever seen."

"Perhaps you should get out more," Sanders replied. "She killed Danilo Lelac in single combat."

"The Golden Wolf?" Hades asked, his eyes bulging with incredulity.

"One and the same."

"Why do I get the feeling I have been deceived?" Hades replied.

"It is you who insisted on this spectacle," Sanders said.

"Very well, "Hades raised his hand back to his throat. "Underworld, are you ready?"

The cheers were deafening.

"As always, the rules of the cage are simple. No magic, your body is your only weapon. Use it how you will. Last man"—Hades looked at Kasey—"or woman standing—wins!"

The crowd bellowed their approval. "Dozer, Dozer, Dozer."

Dozer pushed himself off the wall of the cage and ambled into the center of the confined space. He sized Kasey up and down and let out a snort. Raising his fists, he charged straight at her.

He was going for the quick win. With such an advantage of size, his best hope was to knock her out swiftly before he tired too much.

Kasey had no intention of letting him play his game. As he closed in, Kasey nimbly sidestepped him. She turned as he passed and punched him in the kidneys.

If Dozer felt it, he didn't register the blow. He simply whirled about to face her.

He closed in again and threw a right punch at Kasey's face. Kasey ducked under the blow and delivered one of her own to his ribs before dancing back out of his reach.

As he came at her again, she stepped into him and delivered a thunderous right kick straight to his chest. The kick halted his advance. The muscles in his face contracted in pain as the wind was forced from his lungs. He staggered for a step as he fought to recover his breath.

*So, you can be hurt.*

Seizing the advantage, Kasey threw a left jab toward Dozer's face. As his hands came up to block the maneuver, she pulled back her fake jab and drove another solid right kick into Dozer's exposed chest.

He let out a bellow of rage and lunged at her. His murderous haymaker passed over her head but still he kept coming. Dropping his shoulder, he slammed into her. She dropped to the mat.

Dozer raised both his arms in triumph. The crowd erupted into cheers.

Kasey rolled onto her front and pushed herself to her feet.

Dozer turned to face her, but Kasey was already closing the distance. She rained a series of blows at his chest. The first connected, slipping past Dozer's guard but the rest deflected harmlessly off his raised arms. As Kasey backed away, Dozer swung a wild backhand at her. The blow clipped her shoulder, and her muscles seized in protest.

If it had connected more solidly, she would have been picking herself up off the mat once more.

*I need to slow it down. I have to tire him out.*

Dozer closed with her time and time again, but Kasey just continued circling the cage, dancing back out of his reach.

The crowd booed, but Kasey didn't care. Dozer's energy was starting to wane. He may have been built like a brick wall but he moved like one too. He wouldn't be able to keep up with her forever.

Dozer lunged to his right, cutting off her movement and forcing her back toward the edge of the cage. She tried to back up, but he was already on top of her. He drove home his thunderous punches. Kasey blocked with her arms and dodged where she had room but each hit that connected sent jarring pains shooting through her body.

Her arms felt like one giant bruise that throbbed with each beat of her racing heart. She needed room to breathe, but Dozer wasn't relenting. She stepped past his next punch, and then put everything she could into a solid uppercut straight to Dozer's chin.

His head jerked back, but he simply shrugged it off. He grabbed her by the shoulders and drove her into the corner of the cage.

Kasey knew his plan was to pin her where she couldn't move and then bludgeon her into submission. He had all the subtlety of a rampaging bull.

As she was thrown towards the corner of the cage, she moved in the only direction she had available: up. She slammed the sole of her shoe against the cage wall, then brought up her other leg against the opposite wall. She pushed off, throwing herself back into Dozer.

He stumbled off balance. She swung around and drove her right fist into his already battered jaw.

His head snapped around like a paper plane caught in a cyclone. He tried to steady his feet beneath him, but it was no good. He went down like a sack of bricks.

The crowd murmured in disbelief as their champion hit the mat.

Kasey circled Dozer as he lay face down on the mat.

"Hit him!" Sanders shouted over the din. "This isn't a fair fight."

Kasey approached Dozer, but it was too late.

The burly fighter was already pushing himself to his feet.

As he staggered, Kasey closed and delivered another punishing right kick to his stomach. He raised his head and grinned, grabbing her leg. His left arm caught her behind her knee as his right arm reached under her armpit. With a speed that defied belief, he scooped Kasey off her feet, and spinning, hurled her across the cage.

Kasey's back collided with the steel bars. She fell to the mat in a heap.

She could see the bright lights obscuring her vision. She hurt all over.

Dozer leered at her. "How's that, princess?"

"People better stop calling me that." Kasey panted as she rolled onto her side and swept her leg around.

Her kick caught Dozer behind the knee and stripped his legs from under him. As he crumpled to the floor, she regained her feet. Looming over him, she kicked him in the ribs.

The crowd roared its approval as Dozer grunted in pain.

Kasey kicked him again, but Dozer batted her leg away with enough force she stumbled. Before she caught her balance, he was back on his feet and bearing down on her.

He was red in the face and panting for air but Kasey had no intention of underestimating him again.

As he threw his next jab, Kasey ducked to the right and drove three lightning quick blows into his ribs. On the third, Kasey heard his rib crack. She smiled; that was going to hurt in the morning.

Before she could back away, he grabbed her by her wrist and pulled her close. Wrapping his arms around her, he yanked her off her feet.

Kasey struggled against the vice-like grip but couldn't get any purchase. Her arms were pinned at her side as he crushed the life out of her.

She could feel Dozer's fetid breath against her neck as his biceps crushed her against his chest. The air escaped her lungs, and she couldn't breathe.

She wrapped her arms around Dozer, managing to gain enough of a hold to steady herself. In desperation, she slammed her knee straight into his groin.

He grunted in pain but didn't relent. Kasey felt her world going black.

Drawing on the last of her strength, she drew back and drove her knee home again. This time, Dozer lost his grip, and she slipped free.

She landed on her feet in a crouch. Without hesitation, she exploded upward, thumping her head back into Dozer's chin.

He staggered backward away from her as he fought to regain his composure.

Advancing on him, Kasey raised her fists. Dozer threw a clumsy right hook. It was a desperate attempt to buy himself time to recover. Kasey ducked under the blow, and as she stepped past him, she delivered a kick to his right knee cap. He sank under his own weight.

The crowd gasped as their champion fell to his knees. Kasey circled him warily.

Kasey looked at Hades. His eyes were wide, but the lord of the underworld was not intervening. He simply watched impassively. Dozer was not on his feet, but he wasn't unconscious either.

"No half measures," Kasey told herself.

Stepping toward Dozer, she whipped her right leg around in a devastating round house. The blow connected with his head. His eyes registered the shock as he snapped sideways. He toppled to the mat like a tree being felled. The sound of him striking the cage's floor carried through the underground chamber.

The crowd roared their approval. Kasey circled the fallen fighter. There was no sign of movement. His eyes were closed, and the only motion was the gradual rising and falling of his chest as his ragged breathing persisted.

He was out cold.

Kasey raised her fists in triumph.

Hades approached the cage. With two hands, he gripped the wheel and released the cage's locking mechanism. The steel beams retracted and rolled back into place. The steel door swung outward and Kasey stepped out of the cage.

Hades grabbed her arm and raised it high.

The crowd roared.

"Denizens of the underworld, our new champion!"

Kasey cocked her head toward Dozer. "You better honor our agreement, Hades, or that will be you."

Hades released her wrist. "I'm a man of my word, Jen. We'll take the contract. Now it's just the small matter of settling the price."

"You can talk to him for that," Kasey replied, nodding at Sanders as she descended the stairs. As she passed Hades' pet, she cracked a grin. "Shame it wasn't you in there. That would have been a whole lot more fun."

Before the woman could respond, Kasey shouldered past her.

A flurry of motion caught her attention. She turned to find herself staring down the barrel of a handgun. Hades' pet glowered menacingly as she waved the pistol in Kasey's face. Hades' wide-eyed countenance told Kasey that he wasn't complicit.

"Hades, get your woman under control," Kasey called.

"I could end you right here," The woman sneered.

"You could try," Sanders called, "but if you pull that trigger, everyone in this room dies."

Kasey felt the familiar thrum of arcane energy surging through the room. Turning, she found Sanders' entire frame glowing. White hot light pulsed outward from him.

Hades stared at Sanders.

Kasey glanced back at the pet who was squinting as she struggled against the glare.

"I'm warning you, Hades," Sanders said. "You have three seconds to get that gun out of my wife's face or your precious underworld is going to be remodeled. I'll bring the city down on all of us, I swear!"

Hades grabbed the pistol and yanked it out of his pet's grip. After sliding it back into its holster, he raised his finger to censure her. "Don't ever draw a weapon on our guests again. Normally I find your impetuosity delightful, but today you could get us all killed."

As Hades fastened the holster over his pistol's grip, Sanders gradually released the energy he had been building and storing, allowing it to harmlessly dissipate into the air.

"I believe all that is left to discuss is the price," Sanders said as the last of his energy faded.

Hades strode over to where Sanders waited. "The price is one million. Cash. We'll send a team where and when you ask. I'm sure you'll agree, one man just won't do."

Sanders nodded. "I'll have the cash delivered tomorrow. Have a phone waiting for us, we'll call when we are ready. I'd say it's been a pleasure, but I'd be lying."

Hades leaned closer, so that no one else but Kasey could overhear him. "If I were to cast a revelation spell right now, who would I find standing before me? Not Ben Kaswell, of that I am sure."

Sanders ground his teeth. "I wouldn't if I were you. Whatever happens, I would be sure to kill you first."

Hades smiled, revealing two rows of perfectly straight teeth. "I don't doubt it at all. I just wanted to be sure. It's been a pleasure to meet you, Director Sanders. Or should I just call you Noah?"

Sanders raised his hand, but Hades pushed it down.

"No need for that here. The ADI's influence holds no sway here. Whatever reward they are offering, we couldn't care less. These are strange times indeed, and I find that the enemy of my enemy is now my friend. So go in peace. We will talk again soon, Sanders."

# CHAPTER 11

Kasey's body was on fire. From her head to her feet, everything felt like one enormous bruise. With each beat of her heart, her body throbbed. The fight with Dozer had been more taxing than she had expected. She had spent most of the first day sleeping it off in the hotel room, but now it was time to get her body moving again. She decided to pick up some much-needed supplies.

Slowly but surely, she made her way down the busy streets of Manhattan. All around her, the city was alive. Pedestrians thronged the street, from tourists taking in the Big Apple to business people making their way around town.

Kasey never got tired of the city. Wearing her illusion as a mask, she wandered through the city. It would not serve her to be identified as Kasey Chase. The ADI's misinformation campaign continued to run on TV stations and in the newspaper.

So once more, Kasey was Jen Kaswell. Wearing another's identity was beginning to wear on her. It wasn't just the physical drain of maintaining the illusion, but the emotional drain also. In the last week, she had spent more time as others than she had as herself. There was little choice though—the ADI was relentless.

Reaching the store she sought, Kasey pushed open the glass door and wandered in. The small electronics retailer sat nestled in a series of shops that occupied the first floor of an apartment building. Residential apartments towered overhead, obscuring the afternoon sun that was soon to descend. Behind the desk was a Latino man in his thirties. He was standing behind a display cabinet with a glass top. Along each of the walls rested row upon row of cell phone accessories.

"Can I help you with something?" the clerk asked.

"Sure, I'm looking for a 450 Flip," Kasey said.

The man raised an eyebrow. "Are you sure? We carry the latest smart phones. Why would you want to buy something so ancient? It doesn't even have a camera."

She had to admire the man's roundabout efforts at an up-sell, but in her current state, it was the last thing on her mind.

She approached the counter and leaned on it. "I don't need anything fancy, but I do need a few of them. I won't be using them for long, if you get my drift."

The clerk perked up. "A few of them? Well, I'm sure we can do you a deal if you're buying in bulk."

"You read my mind," Kasey replied. "I'll take six. I need them set up, loaded, and ready to go."

The man smiled, reached beneath the bench, and drew out a box before placing it on the countertop. "Normally, these go for ninety dollars, one-hundred and ten if we do the set up, but for you, my lovely lady, I'll do the six for five-fifty. Would you like them prepaid or on a plan?"

"Prepaid will be fine," Kasey said, reaching into her knapsack, she pulled out several bills and handed them to the clerk. If he had any skepticism about the wad of cash, he kept it to himself.

"I'll just take the phones, too. I have no need for the boxes and one charger should suffice. "

"Very well," the clerk said, picking up the box. "I'll just be a couple of minutes setting things up. Feel free to browse the store or grab a cup of coffee. I'll be with you shortly."

*Coffee. Now there's an idea.*

"I'll be back in ten," she replied, heading for the exit. She pulled open the heavy glass panel door and stepped back onto the street.

She didn't have to go far. Parked on the street corner was a coffee cart. Its barista churned out order after order for the anxious queue that waited for him.

There were a half a dozen people ahead of her in line, not that it mattered. She was in no particular hurry today. She simply needed to get the phones and make her way back to the hotel.

With the ADI stepping up their campaign against her, she had calls to make.

Sanders had observed the ADI watching the 9$^{th}$ Precinct; it was safe to say they were keeping tabs on Kasey's friends and family too. She would need burner phones to keep her communications away from the prying eyes and ears of the ADI.

She'd not spoken to her mother in weeks and knew the ADI's current smear campaign would be taking a toll.

Sanders had mentioned he had a few calls that he wanted to make also. In spite of the ADI's consistent harrying, Sanders remained determined that there were agents still sympathetic to his cause. Sanders was determined to reach out to them in his search for allies.

Kasey took a step forward as yet another patron received their coffee. Sanders had been gone when she woke up. A note on the table told her he'd gone to Hades to make the payment.

At first, Kasey was irritable that she had been left behind, but as she had hobbled around the suite, she had seen the wisdom in his course of action. There was no need for Kasey to ever see Hades and his malicious little pet again. Sanders had likely gone solo to avoid antagonizing the situation further.

Besides, his choice had given her the opportunity to relax and clear her mind. It was a valuable chance to consider the plan ahead. Now that they had secured the support of the Underworld, they still needed an opportunity to take a run at Arthur Ainsley.

He'd not been seen in public since their attack on the ADI. So, Kasey was wanting any lead she could get on his whereabouts. When it came to information on the Shinigami posing as Arthur Ainsley, she had only one card left to play.

*Oh, John.* She was reluctant to call him for many reasons. Ever since their dinner date, she hadn't known how to feel. She had thoroughly been enjoying herself until Sanders had interrupted the evening in spectacular style.

The fact that she had any feelings other than frustration was still something she was trying to come to terms with. The thought of calling him now was causing her heart to race.

How would she explain away the fact that she'd been seen helping Sanders break into the ADI? How could she explain that she was working with the man who was trying to kill his father? How could she explain working with a murderer?

Of course, all of the accusations against Sanders were false, but she was one of the few people alive who knew so. To the rest of the world, Sanders was a wanted criminal. How could she explain to John that the man he was reconciling with wasn't his father at all, but a mass murdering psychopath trying to destroy the city and the lives of millions of people?

She had considered calling him many times, wanting to warn him about how much danger he was in. Each time she had picked up the phone though, Kasey had forced herself to reconsider.

For the time being, John was stuck spending every day with the man posing as his father. If she told John and he slipped, if he gave away any indication of Arthur's true identity, his own life would be in danger. It was better for him if Kasey kept the knowledge to herself.

Now she wondered if she would have any other choice. John would surely demand an answer of her. If she wanted to know where the Shinigami Master posing as his father was, she would need to talk to John.

"I'll cross that bridge when I come to it," Kasey told herself as she stepped up to the coffee cart.

*One problem at a time.*

"What can I get you?" the barista asked with a smile.

"Double shot latte, please," Kasey said.

"And what name should I put that under?"

"Ka... Jen," Kasey replied, having to catch herself.

"Lovely to meet you, Jen. I'll just be a moment." The barrister tinkered away behind his cart. In moments, he was holding a fresh cup of steaming coffee. "Here you go, Jen. That'll be four-fifty."

Kasey drew out her wallet and lifted out a fifty dollar note. The barista nodded as he counted out her change. Palming the change, Kasey pushed the notes and coins into her wallet and took a tight-lipped swig of the hot coffee. The warm brew heated her up from the inside out, and she let out a satisfied, albeit involuntary, moan of delight.

She turned to walk away.

"Have a great day, Jen!" the barista called with a wide smile.

Kasey nodded and made her way back to the electronics store. Entering the shop, she found the clerk waiting for her. Six phones were stacked neatly on the countertop with the charger sitting by them.

"Six phones, one charger, all on prepaid plans, waiting and ready to go." The clerk swept his hand over the phones.

Kasey set down the coffee, then scooped up the phones and dropped them into her knapsack.

"Thank you, that's excellent." As she picked up the charger, the man held out his hand to stop her.

"If you need any others, simply give us a call and I'll have them ready for you."

"Will do. Thanks for the phones." She tossed the charger in the sack and drew out the first phone. As she made her way out of the store, she raised the phone and dialed a number she knew by heart.

The phone rang three times before a familiar voice answered, "Hello?"

Kasey choked back tears. "Hey Mom."

"Kasey?" her mother almost squealed. "Where have you been? I've been worried sick."

Kasey ran one hand through her hair as she clutched the phone in the other. "I have been all over. I'm sorry I haven't called. It wasn't safe. I didn't want to put you or Dad at risk."

"Kasey, what's going on? They are saying the most horrible things about you on the news."

"It's all lies, Mom. Misinformation spread by the council to turn the public against us."

"Us?" her mother asked. "So, you are with him then? Director Sanders? They say he's a killer."

Kasey shook her head. This wasn't going well at all. "That's what I thought too, at first. But it looks like he was being framed. I saw the body and I had a vision. It definitely wasn't him. He's been set up."

"By who?"

"I can't tell you. Not without putting you in even greater danger. Right now, they are only after us. I don't want to drag you into this too."

"I'm your mother. I'm already in this. Whatever this is."

"No, Mom. I just wanted to let you know I was safe. I'm safe and we have a plan to put things back to normal."

"So why are the ADI hunting you, Kasey? They came by the house. They asked if I'd seen you."

"Sorry, Mom, just tell them the truth. You don't know anything, so there's nothing to tell. The ADI are after us because we broke into the Arcane Council."

Her mother's tone grew tenser with every sentence. "The Arcane Council? Kasey, are you crazy? There are wizards who have been killed for less."

"I had to do it, Mom. I needed the truth. There was no other way. At least now we know what we're dealing with. We just need the last few pieces to fall into place."

Her mother drew a deep breath. "Kasey, what are you up to? What are you planning?"

Kasey looked up as she crossed the street. "It's better you don't know. It's better that no one knows. Don't worry, I'll be home soon."

Before her mother could reply, Kasey cut the call and snapped the flip phone in half. She threw both halves into a nearby trashcan and continued walking.

It bothered her that her mother had even asked if she were guilty. Surely, by now, she'd earned the benefit of the doubt.

*She's just worried about me.*

Her mother was amongst the most overprotective women on the planet. She would go to her grave before she let harm come to Kasey. Even grown up, Kasey had never quite been able to slip her mother's watchful eye.

Either way, at least her mother knew she was safe. Hopefully it would all be over soon. With Hades' help and the men he had pledged, shortly the reign of the Shinigami would be brought to an end, and the Arcane Council would be free of their influence.

Sanders certainly seemed confident that without the Shinigami in charge, he would win back control of the ADI. More importantly, the Shinigami plot against the city would be brought to an end. The city would be safe, and the vision that Kasey had witnessed all too often since her twelfth birthday would be a distant memory. It was a sight that she hoped never to see again.

She quickened her pace. Even though she was wearing an illusion, she couldn't help but feel that people were watching her. Being hunted by the ADI had made her paranoid.

Knowing they were willing to kill her on sight had her wired and on high alert, but constantly looking over her shoulder was starting to take a toll on her.

She reached the hotel and slid through the revolving door. Crossing the lobby, she made her way straight for the elevators. Pressing the up arrow, she was relieved when one of the sets of gold leaf doors parted. The elevator was waiting for her.

She stepped inside and punched the button for the penthouse.

The penthouse suite had been a rare treat. A far cry from her dingy apartment, it had certainly been a welcome relief after weeks of staying in dilapidated motels across the city.

The elevator arrived and the doors parted.

As she made her way down the corridor a woman pushing a room service cart was leaving the penthouse.

The woman stepped aside and pushed open the door with her hand.

"I've just finished. If you need anything else, please don't hesitate to call," the woman said.

"Thanks," Kasey replied, slipping past her into the room. After sliding the door closed behind her, she reached for the chain and locked the door. She turned to face the room. "Sanders, are you here?"

No reply was forthcoming. It seemed he hadn't finished with Hades yet.

Kasey worried that the self-elected ruler of the Underworld might have gone back on their deal.

What would she do if Sanders didn't return?

She shook off the thought. It didn't bear thinking about. Their current plan may have been bold and direct, but it was just what was needed. The ADI thought they had them on the run.

A direct assault against the Chancellor after days of fleeing would certainly take them by surprise. The additional manpower Hades had promised had really opened up their options.

There was a knock at the door.

Kasey crossed the room and stared through the peephole. The housekeeper stood at the door with her cart.

"Hello?" Kasey called without opening the door.

"Hi, it's me again. I'm sorry, I think I left my mop in the bathroom. Could I grab it?"

Kasey undid the chain and opened the door.

As the door opened, she saw a shadow fall across the cleaner's face. The shadow was cast by an enormous skinhead in a black leather jacket.

Kasey's mouth began to move, until she spotted the black pistol pointed directly at her chest.

# CHAPTER 12

Kasey stared at the jet-black pistol leveled at her chest. Her mind raced a million miles an hour, but she didn't dare move. At this range, there was no way she would be able to raise a shield in time. She would be shot just like Sanders had been in the Underpass.

Her assailant had the drop on her. If she lowered her hands to make a play for the gun, she was just as likely to catch a bullet.

The thug stared at her intently, his cold steely gaze meeting her own. "Don't even think about it. Just one word and you are dead. I saw the footage from the bunker. If you so much as open your mouth without my say so, I'll kill you. Understood?"

Kasey nodded slowly.

"Inside, now. Both of you."

The thug placed one hand on the housekeeper and forced her inside the room. His hand holding the pistol never deviated from Kasey, not even for a moment.

Kasey backed slowly into the room. The thug followed her inside, closing the door behind him.

"Over there on the couch, both of you. Sit down, slowly. I'm warning you. If you make a move, she'll certainly die." The thug nodded at the housekeeper. "Then you will follow shortly thereafter. Who knows, maybe you'll die first. Just try it and we'll see."

The man was Night Crew. Kasey had no doubt about that. His appearance, the accent, everything pointed toward that certainty.

*But how did he find us here?*

The illusions they had used to shroud their identity should have been more than enough to throw the Night Crew off their trail for good.

*Unless it wasn't us they were following. It must be the money.*

With the volume of cash they had witnessed in the stash house, it made sense that the Night Crew would have some way of tracking their ill-gotten gains. Perhaps some sort of device concealed with the notes themselves.

"I want to know where our money is. All of it. You are either ignorant or have a death wish to steal from the Night Crew." The thug shook his head. "Have you not heard?"

Kasey stared down the thug. "Heard what? That the Night Crew lost millions of dollars, and dozens of men in a single night? No, I hadn't. In fact, I have no idea what you're talking about."

"Don't play with me," the thug threatened. "We have means of making you tell us what we wish to know."

Kasey ran her fingers through her hair. "I have no idea what you're talking about, or what you want to know. I don't even know who you are."

The man reached into his pocket and drew out his cell phone. Setting the cell phone on the coffee table, he slid it in front of Kasey. A map of Manhattan was blown up on the screen. A red dot blinked in exactly the place the hotel occupied.

"I know money is here in this building. The manager was most helpful with my inquiries. There were few couples who checked in the night we were robbed. Of those who checked in, only you were using a false identity. I think we can all agree that this is too great a coincidence to be ignored."

"I'm sorry to disappoint, but that's exactly what it is. A coincidence. You've got the wrong room. I don't know what else I can tell you," Kasey replied.

The thug's finger tightened on the trigger. "You lie to me one more time, and I'm going to put a bullet in you. If you aren't going to tell me where my money is, simply tell me which kneecap you'd prefer to live without."

Kasey was reluctant to give up the hard-won money, but she could see the writing was on the wall. She needed to stall for time. If the thug learned that most of it was already gone, he'd likely shoot them both.

Kasey knew that at any moment, Sanders might return, but until he did, or she saw an opening, she was stuck following the killer's instructions. From the thug's temperament and his cold dead eyes, she doubted he would bat an eyelid before pulling the trigger.

"It's in the safe," Kasey replied. "We couldn't leave that much cash just laying around."

"Get it out," the thug said. "Move slowly or you die. Reach for a weapon and you die. In short, try anything at all—"

"And I die," Kasey finished the sentence. "I think I get it."

She stood slowly, and the thug followed suit.

"Stay there," the thug said to the housekeeper, who still trembled helplessly on the couch.

The housekeeper nodded slowly, avoiding any eye contact with Kasey or the thug.

Kasey shuffled into the bedroom. The thug followed her but hovered at the door, where he could both see Kasey and the housekeeper.

*He's smart.*

She had hoped the opportunity would give the housekeeper a chance to run for her life. Kasey had few qualms about putting down a murderer like the Night Crewman that loomed behind her, but the thought of an innocent woman dying simply because she was in the wrong place at the wrong time was something she wanted to avoid at all costs.

She opened the built-in robe revealing the safe and glanced over her shoulder. The thug hadn't moved, and his weapon was still pointed squarely at her. She wondered if she could raise a shield in time at this distance but drove the thought from her mind. He was still too close and the risk too high. She just needed to stall for long enough for Sanders to arrive. Or, if she could distract the thug for long enough, she might be able to shield herself and retaliate.

The thug might have been immense, but if she could take the gun out of play, it would at least level the playing ground, and give her a chance to use her magic. Her powers were potent, but she had no desire to race a bullet.

"Open it. What are you waiting for?" the thug said.

"Oh, nothing. I just didn't want you getting trigger happy when I reached for the keypad," Kasey replied with a shrug.

"Open it now. I want to see our money."

"Alright, alright." She punched in the combination code. On the fourth digit, the lock clicked and rolled back into the unlocked position.

She pulled open the safe, revealing the black duffel bag she had carried with her from the Night Crew bunker.

"Easy now," the thug called. "Don't give me a reason to shoot you."

She slowly lifted out the duffel. Holding it aloft in one arm, she turned to face him.

"Where do you want it?" she asked.

"Set it on the bed. Then open it slowly."

Kasey gingerly made her way from the safe to the bed and set the duffel on the corner of the mattress.

"Unzip it slowly."

Kasey drew open the zipper and parted the duffel, so that the thug could see the stacked notes inside.

"There you go," Kasey replied. "Obviously, it's short a few dollars for the room."

The thug grinned but there was nothing happy about that smile. It was a sinister sliver of a grin that seemed to perk slightly at the corners of his mouth.

"Our surveillance shows you carrying two bags from the bunker. Where is the second bag?"

"This is all I have," Kasey lied. "I don't know anything about a second bag."

If the thug was expecting it to be in the hotel, then only one of the bags must've had a tracker unit. However the Night Crew had placed the trackers, clearly it was sporadic. Not every stack of bills, would have one. It was fortunate that it was Kasey's bag and not Sanders' that they had tracked. Kasey didn't doubt Hades would have frowned on them leading the Night Crew into the heart of his lair.

The thug exhaled slowly.

"There were two bags. That is only one. Tell me where the other is, or I'll shoot you." His voice grew in volume with each sentence.

"I'm telling you, that's all I have," Kasey replied. "You can see the safe, look for yourself. There's nothing else in there."

"I can see that," the thug snapped. "I can see that it is empty. I want to know where the money is and I want to know now!"

He advanced on her, gun still at the ready. "Tell me, or I'll put a bullet in that pretty face of yours."

The sound of footsteps from the adjoining room took them both by surprise.

*The housekeeper is making a dash for it.*

As the thug turned and bolted for the adjoining room, the hotel room door opened. She charged around the corner as the thug raised his pistol to fire. Without hesitation, she dove after him. With both hands, she grabbed the outstretched, pistol shoving it to the side.

Time seemed to slow as the thug's finger squeezed the trigger. The shot flew wide, slamming into the wall next to the door. The housekeeper screamed as she ran for her life. Kasey and the thug collapsed in a heap on the hotel room floor.

Kasey hit the ground hard. Wincing in pain, she forced her mind to focus. Her bruises from the night before with Dozer were still fresh. She closed her eyes and shut out the pain. Only one thing mattered now, and that was the gun in the thug's hand. She knew that if she let go of the gun, it would be the last thing she ever did.

She wrapped herself around his arm and kicked him in the ribs. He jerked back, and she changed her grip. Pointing the gun clear of herself, she squeezed down on the trigger.

Shots hammered past her, into the hotel wall. She continued jerking the trigger.

A hollow click signaled the last round had been fired.

Safe from imminent death, she grabbed the thug's wrist and slammed it into the floor. As his fingers loosened, she twisted his wrist in on itself and the gun came free. She picked up the gun and raised it, ready to pistol whip him.

He reached over with his other meaty arm, grabbing her with both hands, and rolled, throwing her as he went. She slammed into the table in the suite.

Like a cat, she rolled to her feet as the thug struggled to his own. She grabbed one of the hardwood chairs and swung it with all her might. The chair struck the thug and broke across his flank. Still he came on, charging like a bull.

He grabbed her, lifting her off her feet, and slammed her down onto the tabletop. Kasey felt her head slam against the wood, almost losing consciousness.

*Oh, no.*

With only moments before the thug crushed the life out of her, she placed her palm on his chest. *"Poen."*

As the words passed her lips, the thug's face twisted in horror.

Before Kasey could finish her spell, he released her and drove his right fist straight into her guts. Kasey doubled over in pain as the punch forced the air from her lungs. Gasping for breath, she fought back tears.

The thug reached for her again. She drove her right leg into his ribs, but he shook her off and grabbed her throat.

His hands closed around her windpipe, choking the life from her.

*If I can't speak, I can't use my magic, and if I can't use my magic, I'm dead.*

The exhaustion of the recent days threatened to overwhelm her. On a good day, she might have given the thug a run for his money, but today she was tired and worn down.

She felt the life being forced from her.

As her world went black, something stirred within her. It wasn't magic; this was no whispering of the arcane ready to aid her. No, this was much older than that. It was a throbbing sensation, resonating from deep within her soul. The primal manifestation of her inner feelings. It was an emotion that had plagued mankind since the beginning.

It was rage. Kasey was furious at everything that had brought her to this point. Furious at the Shinigami and their foul plot. Furious at the ADI who hunted her. Furious that she'd been driven to fight for her life in a cage to amuse others, furious that she'd had to go toe to toe with a criminal syndicate just to stay alive, and furious that their hired gun was right now squeezing the very life out of her.

Today, that rage was her ally.

She struggled as the thug's grip tightened around her throat. Her hands raced across the table top as she searched for anything she could use. At last, her fingers found purchase. She felt the cool stone of a ceramic bowl resting in the middle of the table. Grabbing it with both hands, she heaved it off the table and into the thug's head.

As the ceramic antique shattered against his skull, his grasp on her loosened. She rolled free, then kicked the man in his face.

Doubling over, she sucked in a deep breath, filling her lungs with much-needed oxygen. Her chest burned but so did her anger.

The thug reached for something inside his jacket. Kasey slid off the table as the thug drew out a blade. It was long and slender, some sort of switchblade. The light in the room flickered off its keen edge.

The thug lunged forward, slashing at her. Kasey leapt backwards, and the slender blade sliced through the air, barely missing her stomach.

Flicking his wrist, the thug changed his grip and swung the blade once more. This time, the strike was higher, towards Kasey's neck. She ducked underneath the blade and drove a solid right into the man's throat.

The thug gasped for air. As he did, she reached for his wrist and in one deft motion turned it in on itself. As his wrist gave under the pressure, the blade dropped from his hand. Kasey caught it in her right hand, flipped it, and sunk the blade into the thug's chest.

As the blade drove home, she felt sick to her stomach. She'd inflicted pain before, but this reminded her of Danilo Lelac whom she had impaled on the Spear of Odin. The feel of a blade breaking flesh wasn't a sensation she enjoyed at all.

The thug's eyes went wide, as his blood pooled. He clutched both hands to his chest in an effort to stem the flow.

Kasey grabbed him and shoved him backward onto the sofa.

The thug growled in pain as he hit the cushion. His hands closed around the knife as he made to pull it out.

"I wouldn't be doing that," Kasey warned, wiping blood from her mouth. "Pull it out and you'll bleed to death. Leave it in there and there is still a chance you might survive long enough for the paramedics to get you to a hospital. Doubtless this racket has already been reported to the police, they will be on their way, so it's your choice. Follow me or live to fight another day."

She made her way over to the duffel and drew out the stacks of bills. Checking each one at a time, she set aside several that had trackers hidden inside the wads of cash. She threw the clean stacks back in the duffel and shouldered the bag. As she made her way through the suite, she caught the Night Crewman staring her down.

"Don't be so disheartened," she said with a shrug, "this could have gone much worse for you."

The man struggled to speak. "When my employer finds you, he will kill you."

"He'll have to get in line," Kasey replied, "and that list gets longer every day. If I'm gonna be honest, your boss is the least of my worries right now. I left some of the cash on the bed as a consolation prize. Tell him to take it and cut his losses. If I see any of you again, we'll burn another stash house to the ground and another and another. We'll continue until you decide to leave us alone or kill us. Either way, it's going to be bad for business, so you decide, but I have other, more pressing issues I need to focus on."

With that, she hurried out of the penthouse. She hit the elevator's call button, and a moment later, the gilded doors parted. She stepped inside. Taking care not to stare at the camera, she instead stood beneath its arc of vision.

The illusion she'd been utilizing for the past few days wouldn't serve her now. Jen Kaswell was as good as dead. As soon as the police arrived, she would be a wanted woman. Whispering her incantation, she shifted her appearance once more.

As the elevator reached the lobby, Kasey stepped off. Her new face meant she could walk straight through the lobby without suspicion. No doubt the hotel security was already responding to the disturbance. As they bustled about, Kasey crossed the lobby and stepped onto the street. Lights and sirens signaled the approach of the police.

Kasey strode down the busy New York street, leaving the chaos and the carnage of the penthouse suite behind her.

As the emergency service vehicles rolled past, Kasey reflexively looked away. It took a moment to remember that they would have no chance of connecting the face she now wore with what had transpired in the hotel room, or with her own appearance for that matter.

Reaching into the duffel bag, she drew out another burner phone and dialed the number for Sanders' last remaining burner. With the hotel room being compromised, she needed to make sure he didn't walk straight back into the waiting arms of the police, or worse yet, the ADI.

They avoided using it where possible but now it was a matter of life or death. Kasey dialed the number and waited.

The dial tone repeated tediously in her ear.

"Come on, Sanders, pick up," Kasey muttered as she made her way down the street

"Hello?" Sanders asked, answering at last.

"Hey, it's your wife," Kasey said. "How did your visit with our friend downstairs go?"

"Well, from the look on his face, I'm thinking he didn't expect us to be able to come up with the money, but he assures us he is good to his word. He promised us the use of eight of his men. Turns out he's a little invested in upsetting the Arcane Council."

"Excellent," Kasey said. "Where are you now?"

"On the way back to the hotel, why?" Sanders replied.

Kasey fidgeted with the duffel bag as she walked. "You can't go back there. It's burned."

"What happened?" Sanders asked with concern.

"Turns out, those stacks of cash we looted from the Night Crew had trackers in them. At least my bag did, anyway. One of their enforcers paid me a visit."

"Kasey, are you okay?"

Kasey bit her lip. "I'm okay, I guess. It's just been, well, you know. I guess I was just hoping I could take a nap and not come face-to-face with a hired killer."

"You're not okay. I get it," Sanders said. "Where are you? I'll come to you."

"I'm alright. It was just close, that's all. He certainly got the worse end of the deal. I left him in the suite bleeding all over the sofa. I think it's safe to say we won't be getting our security deposit back. I find it a little ironic that the damages are going to be paid for out of the money the Night Crew sent him to retrieve."

Sanders laughed. "Just a bit. Where are you headed now?"

Kasey looked up to see Central Park looming up ahead. She had to clear her mind and a little nature would serve her well.

"I'm just headed to the park to relax and catch my breath. Besides, I still haven't had a chance to locate our friend. All the allies in the world won't do us much good unless we can find our target. I'm about to make some calls to see what I can dig up."

"Okay, sounds good. Rest up and stay safe. Let me know when you want to meet up. We'll find somewhere quiet we can crash for the night."

Kasey nodded. "Sounds good. I'll see you soon."

Kasey cut the call but didn't put the phone away. She still had one more call to make. They needed the Chancellor's whereabouts and there was no way anyone else in the Arcane Council would be willing to speak to her.

She called the one person on earth she thought might still give her the time of day. Slowly, she punched the number into a cell.

The phone rang twice before it was picked up.

A man's voice carried down the line. "Hello, this is John."

# CHAPTER 13

Kasey stood there on the busy New York street, John's voice echoing in her ear. She knew she had to make the call and yet no matter how much she had thought about it, she still didn't know what to say. How would she explain being with Sanders? How could she protect John from the knowledge that his father was dead, and the Shinigami impostor was sharing his dinner table?

"Hello?" John said. "Is anyone there?"

Kasey exhaled slowly. "John, it's me, Kasey."

"Kasey, where are you? Are you ok?

"John, I can explain everything. It's not easy, though. It's a long story. I need you to hear me out."

"I'll say," John replied with a groan. "You told me someone was going to try and kill my father in the cathedral and then you disappear only to be seen days later carving a path through the Arcane Council with the traitor, Sanders. How could you do that, Kasey? How could you work with him after everything he did to Theo? After everything he did to me? That attack on the manor. He could have killed me."

It was everything Kasey was afraid off. John had so many questions. And most of the answers would put John squarely in the firing line.

"It's not like that, John," Kasey replied. "Sanders didn't kill Theo. I can tell you that much. We only broke into the Arcane Council so that I would be able to examine the body and get to the bottom of all this."

John's temper flared as his tone rose. "I see he got to you, Kasey. Sanders was always a persuasive one. How did he get to you?"

"It's not important right now, John. I just called to talk. I wanted to tell you that I was okay, and that I was making progress in finding the Getz killer. The Council is after Sanders and now they're after me. They're barking up the wrong tree. I just wanted to make sure you knew, because the real killer is still out there. They are a danger to you, your family, the Council, everything! John, whatever you think of me, don't let your guard down with anyone else. I believe the killer is inside the Council. We know that much. They are using their resources to cover themselves and blame Sanders. It's just a distraction to throw everyone off the scent. We're getting close, we just need a little more time."

"More time, Kasey. This is insane. Have you seen the news? They're saying you killed a bunch of tenants in some building downtown. What the hell is going on?"

"More lies, John. I thought you knew me better than that. The building we hit was a drug house run by one of the local gangs. We needed some resources. With the ADI breathing down our neck, we couldn't afford to go to anyone. So, we borrowed a little cash from someone who shouldn't have had it in the first place."

"A regular Robin Hood." He let out an exasperated sigh. "What is it you want, Kasey? Why call now?"

"Like I said, John. I just wanted to warn you, let you know I was okay. I'm sorry that I disappeared without saying anything. There wasn't time and frankly, the last few days I've been fighting for my life."

"Sounds about right, but I'm betting you need something. You only seem to remember my number when you need something. Like info on the council, my dad, or some case. Just leave me out of it, okay? Whatever crusade you and Sanders are on, leave me out of it."

The blow struck home. Kasey knew he was right, and it hurt. She'd taken him for granted and called for a favor one too many times. It was bad timing and she knew it. But, in spite of everything, her warning was genuine. She wanted him to be safe and right now, no one was in more danger than him, mere paces from the master of a death cult bent on the destruction of the city. If John discovered his father had been replaced by the Master of the Shinigami, he would end up just like Getz.

Kasey wasn't willing to risk it.

"John, it's not like that. I called because I didn't want anything to happen to you. You might have trouble believing that. After all, you have the ADI protecting you. They aren't hunting you with a license to kill. In the last few days, I've been beat, raided, shot at, threatened. I was nearly murdered by a mob enforcer this morning. I haven't even stopped to stitch myself up, and here I am, calling you to try and keep your sorry ass safe. I guess this is the thanks I get. It's probably about what I deserve after everything I've screwed up."

She took a deep breath. "Look, John, my timing might be worthless, but at least take a moment to see how wrong you are. You might not believe me but turn on the news. Doubtless there will be coverage of a thug being wheeled out of the Hyatt with a knife lodged in his chest. He's the man who was trying to kill me only minutes ago. Whatever you think I've done to wrong you, rest assured I'm doing the best I can in a crap situation. I haven't tried to hurt you since the day I broke three of your ribs. If you can't see past that, I get it. But if you can, I'd like to talk. I'd like to see you."

There was a heavy silence at the end of the phone

"John, are you still there?"

"Where, Kasey? I'll come to you."

Kasey knew it was as good as she was going to get. Hopefully she could get the truth out of John without having to tell him everything, but it wasn't going to happen without seeing him. The phone just wasn't going to cut it.

"Central Park. The jogging circuits. Come on your own, John. I'll find you."

"I'll be there soon."

Kasey wound her way through Central Park. In her disguise, there was little chance of being recognized but still, she preferred to meet John somewhere neutral. She wandered along the paths until she found a bench that was shielded by the surrounding greenery and took a seat.

As she waited, she replayed the earlier conversation with John in her head. He was upset and she could see why, but it wasn't as if she had been wantonly trying to cause him harm. More than anything, he seemed blinded by her connection to Sanders, which was understandable after Sanders' attack on the manor. John had spent the night in the Administorum. Magic may have healed his physical wounds, but it appeared the brush with death had left a different kind of scar.

Kasey wondered just how she was going to get him to disclose the Chancellor's whereabouts. Asking about Arthur directly would surely raise his suspicions. She couldn't share her plan with him. If he knew the truth, he was liable to do something rash, and him dealing with the Master of the Shinigami on his own was an unhealthy proposition.

No, she would have to extract the Chancellor's whereabouts far more subtly than that.

When she had visited the manor, the ADI had been keeping both John and Arthur there. There was safety in numbers and combining their protective details made sense. She thought it likely that the two might both be sheltering in the Arcane Council. After their incursion, security had definitely been raised. Kasey didn't relish the thought of another direct assault on Council Headquarters. They had barely made it out alive the last time. The only reason they had stood a chance was that they had taken the ADI by surprise. They wouldn't get that luxury a second time.

She wondered if John would bring his detail with him. They would certainly pose a challenge for her. John had managed to give them the slip once before, and she knew that he would do so again.

As she pondered her choices, the familiar figure of John Ainsley strode down the path. He was scanning the park, likely looking for her. His gaze locked on her for a moment then darted away.

Kasey smiled. If the illusion was good enough to conceal her identity from John who was actively searching for her and knew where to look, it boded well for her ability to evade others.

She stood up and fell into line behind him. Lengthening in her pace, she sought to catch up with him. She glanced over her shoulder. There didn't appear to be any sign of his ADI escort.

If John was willing to leave them behind, it showed that he still had some degree of trust in her. If he feared for his life, then he would likely have brought them along.

As she reached him, she whispered just loud enough for him to hear, but quiet enough that the other pedestrians had no idea what she was saying. "Keep walking, John. Don't look back."

"Kasey, is that you?" In spite of the warning, John looked over his shoulder.

Kasey shook her head. "I told you not to look. People could be watching."

John forced his eyes back to the path ahead and continued walking. "I would never have recognized you. I thought using magic to alter to your appearance is illegal?"

Kasey brushed her blonde hair out of the way. "It is, but with the ADI hunting me, this is the lesser of two evils. It might be breaking the law, but it buys me enough time to stay ahead of them."

"Then why bother meeting me? Surely this puts you at even greater risk," he said.

"I wanted to see you, but I wasn't sure if you'd be able to slip your detail, so I used an illusion. Don't worry, though, no one is hunting Lisa Strauss."

"Lisa Strauss? Who on earth is that?"

"Just some lady I ran into in a hotel the other day. I figured hers was as good an identity as any. She was a normal, so the ADI won't look at me twice."

John shook his head. "This is madness, Kasey. How long do you think you can keep this up for?"

Kasey lengthened her stride so that she was almost beside him. "I don't need to keep this up for much longer at all. We've almost got Theo's killer. As soon as we do, Sanders will be cleared, and everything should go back to normal. If we can get the ADI to stop hunting us, I can go back to my life. This isn't what I want, John."

They wound their way along Central Park's jogging path. Kasey eagerly scanned her surroundings, looking for anyone paying them undue attention. There were hundreds of other exercise enthusiasts out and about. Some stretched as they took a break, others worked their way along the parks' circuits. Nearby, on a patch of lawn, a pair lay sleeping under a tree. No one seemed to give them a second thought.

"What is it you want, Kasey?" John asked. "You called me out of the blue after days of nothing. What's going on?"

"I just wanted to see that you're okay. In spite of everything you seem to think of me, I do care about your well-being. I wanted to make sure you are alright."

"Sanders hasn't tried to kill me recently, if that's what you're referring to. I guess I have you to thank for that?"

Kasey gritted her teeth "He wasn't trying to kill you at the manor. His spell just got out of control."

"Could have fooled me," John replied with an edge. "If you knew Sanders is leaving me alone, then why would I be in any danger?"

"Theo's killer is still out there. It isn't Sanders, but the threat is very real. We're making progress in catching them. It's why we broke into the ADI. I needed to see the body to see if I would have a vision."

John slowed his pace, almost stopping. And did you?"

"Yes," Kasey replied. "It's how I know Sanders didn't do it."

"Then who did?"

Kasey shook her head. "I can't tell you. It's not safe. If I tell you and you say something, anything at all, you'll be dead like Theo and twice as quick. You're safer not knowing for now, while we deal with the killer."

John stopped, whirling around to face her. "How is that your call, Kasey? You ditched me and ran off chasing a killer. Theo was my friend. I have a right to know who killed him."

Kasey looked in John's eyes. He was hurting and frustrated.

"I know, John, but I couldn't bear it if anything happened to you. We are so close to ending this, all we need is a little more time." She paused. "A little more time, and I'll tell you everything. Just make sure that you stay safe. Stay with your detail, be surrounded by as many people as you can. Make sure that no one gets a chance to do you harm."

Her mind raced as an idea presented itself. "Come to think of it, you should stick with your father. The Chancellor's security detail is substantial. There is no safer place than at his side. Speaking of your dad, is he safe?"

"Yeah, he's fine. Since the cathedral, there have been no other attempts on his life. He is holed up in council headquarters. He hasn't left in days. With Sanders on the run, I believe he is personally heading up the task force to catch you both."

Hearing that the Master was hiding in the council headquarters was a blow. Doubtless Arthur had upgraded and changed the security protocols. If they were to succeed in killing the impostor, they would need to lure him out of the council headquarters and make the attempt outside.

"I need you to keep our conversation to yourself, John. Particularly don't tell your father. We are so close to clearing our names, we can't afford to be caught now."

"I wasn't planning on telling him we'd met, Kasey. I just wanted to see you and hear your side of things. I just couldn't understand how you could team up with Sanders after the attack on the manor."

"I told you, it's not like that. Sanders was just trying to get your father to call off the hounds, so that he could clear his name. Now we're forced to do it the hard way with the Arcane Council and the ADI hunting us like rats."

"When does it end? When can we put all of this nonsense behind us?"

"As soon as we catch the killer. Then Sanders can have his job back and I can go back to my life." She stood there, looking at John's expectant face. "I'm sorry, John. I mean it. I didn't want to put you through any of this." She reached out and took his hand in her own. "This isn't how I thought anything would happen. I'm sorry. Just be patient with me, please."

John's pensive expression softened, and the corners of his mouth turned up almost into a smile.

She caught his stare. His warm brown eyes bored into her own, as if he could see into her soul. She wanted to linger, but knew she had to get moving. The knowledge that they needed to bait the Shinigami into the open meant it would take time for them to plan. Hades' hit men wouldn't wait forever.

But right now, in this moment with John, the world seemed to stand still. Her worries all seemed to melt away as he held her hands in his.

Tearing her eyes from his, Kasey saw a woman pushing a stroller toward them. Something seemed off. The woman bopped along to the music playing through her earphones. Kasey's gazed settled on the earphones, and she realized what had drawn her attention. Tucked behind the woman's ear was an earpiece.

Kasey glanced over her shoulder. The man lying underneath the tree had his eyes open now and was looking at her. She couldn't see the earpiece from where she was standing but she suspected he wore one also.

She turned back to John, narrowing her eyes. "John, what is this?"

"What are you talking about?" he asked, forehead creased.

"Did you tell anyone you were coming to meet me?"

"I didn't tell anyone anything!" John replied. "I swear."

Kasey's gaze darted around, and she caught sight of another jogger making their way along the path towards them. Kasey scanned the undergrowth, and in the distance, she could see two men in suits crossing through the park. Another two closed in from the north.

It was the ADI. They were here.

She looked for an exit, but as one, the other park goers turned on her.

*They were all ADI.*

She was sure of it now. Whether on purpose, or inadvertently, John that led her straight into a trap. One that was closing in by the second.

"Kasey, what's going on?" John asked. "What are you looking at?"

"The ADI. They're here. They are everywhere. They must know who I am, or at least suspect it. You led them straight to me."

"Kasey, I would never do that to you. You have to believe me," John pleaded.

"It doesn't really matter now," Kasey replied. "They're here all the same."

She let go of John's hand, turned, and ran.

# CHAPTER 14

Kasey ran for all she was worth. As her feet pounded the pavement, her mind raced.

*How had they found her so quickly? If it wasn't John, then what had given her away?*

Was it possible that they had followed him without his knowledge? He certainly seemed legitimately surprised by their presence.

The park seemed to come to life around her, and Kasey realized the enormity of the trap that had been laid. The jogger running toward her had his eyes locked on her as he reached behind his back.

Kasey had to assume he was armed, and that he was in fact ADI. She swung with all her might. Before the man's hand cleared his back, her right fist caught him in the jaw. He went down like a sack of bricks. As he rolled onto his stomach, Kasey saw the holster that was hidden in the small of his back.

*Good instincts.*

They had kept her alive for weeks, why start doubting them now? She couldn't check if he was unconscious. She had to keep running. The cordon of agents closed on her, but she pressed on. If she could slip through the net, there was a chance she could escape into the city. All she had to do was slip out of sight for long enough to change her appearance and she would be free once more.

Two agents in suits stepped out of the foliage. Their weapons were drawn. Kasey expected to hear the report of the gun shot at any moment. The Shinigami masquerading as Arthur Ainsley had been more than clear with his directive. They could shoot her on sight and face no recourse.

The man hesitated.

Kasey sprang forward. Summoning her power, she chanted, *"Daeargyn!"*

The shock wave rippled outward from her like the epicenter of an earthquake. The two agents were cast aside like rag dolls.

Kasey left the path and went cross-country. Her breathing grew heavier with each loping stride. All about her, there was movement, but there was no time to stop and assess her options. Her one hope lay in breaching the perimeter before they could bring their numbers to bear.

As she ran, another agent stepped out from behind a nearby tree, attempting to clothesline her as she ran past. Kasey ducked under his arm and delivered a blow straight to the man's kidney. He stumbled and fell, sprawling onto the grass.

Kasey ran on, her heart racing. She could feel her pulse pounding in her ears with every step she took.

*Why aren't they shooting me?*

Then it struck her. She was alone. If they shot her, there was no way to gather information on Sanders' whereabouts. It seemed they were intending to take her alive so they could interrogate her. Knowing they were trying to take her alive gave her confidence.

It seemed they were still hesitant to use magic in the midst of so many potential onlookers. Kasey didn't share their hesitation. After all, she was fighting to survive.

She glanced over her shoulder to see a man in a suit running after her. She lengthened her stride, but he gained on her. She darted through Central Park's dense foliage. As her pursuer reached the bushes, Kasey chanted an incantation.

At her command, the shrubbery behind her took on a life of its own and started to grow. Thick vines and branches snapped at the agent, coiling around his limbs and dragging him down, trying to root him to the spot.

Kasey grinned as the man fought back against the vegetation. With a nod, Kasey sent one of the low hanging branches sweeping towards his legs. The bough knocked him off his feet and soon he was entirely incapacitated by the entangling shrubbery.

Kasey broke into a clearing. Two more agents closed in.

Kasey sucked in a deep breath. Her legs were burning with every stride. The exertion in the hotel room had already drained much of her energy. She had not been prepared for her current predicament.

She raised her hands and chanted, "*Trydan!*"

Lightning arced from her outstretched palm toward the two ADI agents. The first raised his hands and shouted in a language Kasey didn't recognize. The blue barrier that materialized before them was all too familiar.

Kasey's lightning played across the surface before earthing itself in the dirt at his feet.

The man's partner countered with a spell of her own. "*Lumiere Aveuglante!*"

The French syllables rolled elegantly off her tongue as a blinding glare emanated from her.

Kasey shielded her eyes, but it was too late. Everything went white.

She was blind.

She tried to shake away the brilliant light that seemed to have seared itself into her retinas. Amid the chaos, she could hear the sound of footsteps approaching.

"Over here, quick," a man said. "We have her now."

Kasey blinked furiously, but to no avail. She opened her eyes but all she could see were colors swimming before them. A series of footsteps to her right warned her that someone approached.

Kasey took a chance and cast her spell blindly, in an effort to deter them. "*Chwyth Aer.*"

The concussive blast rolled from her outstretched palm. Kasey may have fired blind, but she was rewarded with a satisfying yelp of surprise as it struck one of the agents. The agent collapsed. Kasey strained to hear any other signs that might warn her of the nearby agents.

A shuffle to her left came too late. An agent slammed into her torso, throwing her to the ground. Fortunately, the grass was soft and Kasey took the worst of the blow on the right shoulder. The agent's arms wrapped around her as he tried to wrestle her arms behind her back. Kasey rolled against the agent and then away, trying to pitch the agent off her.

The agent managed to stay atop her but lost his grip on her arms. Kasey rolled onto her back and slammed her foot into the agent's groin.

The man groaned as he rolled off her. Kasey felt a little sorry for him. After years in the ring, she could put immense force behind the blow. Much harder, and his likelihood of having children would have diminished severely.

Kasey's vision began to clear as she struggled to her feet. Voices all around her told her she was surrounded. She ran only to be confronted by a haze of shapes before her. More than a handful of ADI agents in suits, if she had to hazard a guess.

"Miss Chase," a man's voice bellowed. "We have you completely surrounded. Surrender yourself and no further harm will come to you. If you continue to resist, we will respond with prejudice."

Kasey whirled about. More shapes closed in behind her. Her eyes could barely see. From the little detail she could make out, she knew her position was growing increasingly tenuous by the second.

She cursed her luck. Despite the immensity of Central Park, she had failed to shake them. Now she was cornered like a rat in a trap. She had no way of getting a message to Sanders in time. Her heart sank as she realized that for the first time in weeks she was truly alone.

The agent's voice rang out once more. "Miss Chase, I'm warning you. Lay face down on the ground and surrender yourself immediately. You won't be warned again."

Kasey raised her arms in surrender, looking about for the source of the voice.

"Get down on the ground, Miss Chase."

Kasey nodded. The agents were closing in all around. They were everywhere.

"That's it, Miss Chase. Face down on the ground."

Lowering her arm as if to place it on the earth, Kasey dropped to one knee. As she did, she summoned the last of her strength, Kasey bellowed, "*Daeargryn.*"

She slammed her fist into the earth with devastating fury.

The pristine manicured grass of Central Park was ripped asunder. Waves of seismic activity radiated out from her. Arcane energy coursed through the earth, splitting it open.

Great chasms opened in the earth, flinging soil and grass. Agents panicked as they were blown about by the energy. As her vision cleared, she could make out the wall of agents scrambling to grab get hold of anything they could, several clinging to the boughs of trees while others had been cast free blown through the air.

Kasey grit her teeth and channeled her will outward, sending the arcane energy farther afield. All about her, Central Park was being torn apart. Trees were uprooted violently like weeds in a giant flowerbed.

She released her spell and took a breath. Looking east, she could see the buildings that lay just beyond the park's edge. She needed to get back to the street, so that she could lose herself in the crowd.

She took off through the devastated park.

She hadn't gone three steps when a voice behind her called, *"Crypelnes."*

The voice was almost on top of her. She had no time to react as the impact of the spell struck her. Her entire body seized up. The sensation started in her spine and spread throughout her limbs. Her legs felt like stone as she collapsed to the earth. She landed on her side, her momentum causing her to roll onto her back. Even as she did, she could feel the sensation spreading. She willed her limbs to move but they would not.

Her whole body felt like it had been encased in concrete.

Whatever spell the agent had used, she was completely paralyzed.

"Miss Chase," the agent called. "We gave you a chance to come peacefully. You should have taken it."

Kasey struggled but it was useless. The veins in her neck felt like they would explode at the exertion, but her limbs wouldn't respond at all. Her eyes darted about but no other part of her body would move.

"You can stop struggling, Miss Chase. The Arcane Council will decide your fate now."

The agent's face came into focus.

Kasey's lip shook with rage. It was Kazinsky.

He smirked down at her. "I think a little rest will do you good." Raising his hand, he chanted. *"Awefecung."*

Kasey felt the spell roll through every joint and muscle. Her body went limp. Against her wishes, her eyes fell shut and the world went black, as her consciousness drifted away.

# CHAPTER 15

Kasey's head ached, as if her brain threatened to explode at any moment. The rest of her felt like she'd fallen asleep on a freeway and been run over by a truck.

Her mind was foggy, but slowly everything was coming back to her. John, her flight through Central Park, and the clash with the ADI. She recalled the paralysis that had held her helpless.

Slowly, Kasey flexed her hands and then her feet. The spell that had held her fast had begun to fade. As her eyes adjusted to the dim light, she found herself lying flat on her back on the cold stone floor.

The steady clink of steel against steel filled her ears. Looking at her hands, she realized they were shackled. A sturdy wrought iron chain joined the shackles on her hands to another set on her feet. A further length of chain ran through a large iron ring set into the stone floor.

The ADI weren't taking any risks.

Desperate for some relief from her aching head, Kasey raised both hands to her temples and muttered a healing incantation, *"Gwella."*

She heard the spell roll off her tongue but felt nothing.

She had expected a brilliant yellow glow, followed by sweet relief, but it didn't happen.

"Your magic is of no use to you here, Miss Chase. Those manacles will see to that."

The lilting air of superiority was all too familiar. Even without seeing him, Kasey knew exactly who it was, the Master of the Shinigami masquerading as Arthur Ainsley.

Slowly, she sat up. It felt like her body was underwater. The aftereffects of the paralysis spell was probably still wearing off. Searching the darkness, Kasey hunted for her foe.

For the first time, Kasey could see her surroundings clearly. She was in a steel cage. It was a dozen paces across. A simple aluminum toilet occupied one corner with a sink beside it. Kasey looked to her left and then her right. There were more cells in each direction. Identical to hers, they stretched into the darkness as far as she could see. All were empty. As far as she could tell, she was the only occupant.

"Why stand there waiting in the dark?" she said. "I'm sure you have been dying to gloat."

At last she had him within reach. Mere feet were all that separated them but it may as well have been miles for all she could do. Locked inside the cell with her magic neutralized by whatever enchantment the cuffs possessed, she was at his mercy.

Knowing the perilous nature of her position, Kasey chose to hide her knowledge of his true identity. Were she to reveal his true identity, she knew her life expectancy would be measured in moments. No, it was definitely best to play it cool. After all, the Master of the Shinigami still had no idea just how much or how little she knew.

The figure strode forward out of the darkness. The all too familiar face of Arthur Ainsley was twisted into a smile that was neither comforting nor congenial. Every part of it made her skin crawl.

Ainsley came to a halt as he reached the bars of the cell.

"Why, Miss Chase, we're delighted to have you here as our guest. I must confess, I didn't think you would stick around. With all the cash you stole from the Night Crew, why stay in the city?"

Kasey held the stare. "I know what you mean, Arthur. The overcrowded subway, traffic so bad you can walk quicker than you can drive. There were a lot of reasons to want to leave but what can I say. I just love the pizza here. Then again, maybe I had some unfinished business. I guess there are some mysteries in life that we'll never know the answer to."

"I wouldn't be so sure, Miss Chase. We have ways of making you talk. If you aren't helpful of your own accord, we'll still get what we want. I just can't guarantee what state you will be in when we are done."

"Oh, you're going to try good cop now, Arthur? It wasn't too long ago you were ordering my execution. What's changed? I imagine I've accumulated quite the list of crimes against the Council. I doubt I'll live through this little vacation. So why should I tell you anything?"

Arthur smiled. "That's where you are wrong, Miss Chase. Yes, you've certainly proved a nuisance these past few weeks, but I'm willing to consider you an unwitting stooge in Sanders' plot. It won't be difficult for the others to believe you were being manipulated by Sanders. I'll even testify on your behalf to the Council. These cells need not be your final resting place. There is no need to spend your remaining years in this sorry hall with naught but your thoughts for company. The real question is, will you help us, or will you waste away your life, which—let's face it—with the list of crimes you've been party too, and my voice speaking against you at sentencing, could be brutally short, indeed."

"So, what? I give you Sanders in exchange for a reduced sentence?" Kasey asked.

Even as the words left her mouth, she could recall the times she and Bishop had delivered a similar offer. Facing jail cracked most petty criminals, and bargaining was one of the most useful tools in their arsenal. It almost always yielded results.

Unfortunately for Arthur Ainsley, she was no common criminal.

"Nice try, Arthur. You've used your position on the Council to try and manipulate me before. You forced me to go after Danilo Lelac, and when all was said and done, was I left alone? No. You've manipulated and harassed me at every opportunity. No deal. Sanders will come for you and you'll be up for early retirement, via the grave."

Arthur hovered beyond the steel poles of the cell. He was almost within reach. If it weren't for the chain fixing her to the floor, she'd have just about been able to punch his sneering face.

"Come on, Kasey. There is no need to languish down here. I could have you out of here in a matter of months. Why throw your life away for Sanders? What has he ever done for you?"

She would never sell out a friend. It didn't matter what was on offer.

She thought of the last few weeks she'd spent with Sanders. More than once, he'd put his life in danger to save hers. She had no doubt that if their situations were reversed, he'd do anything to keep her safe.

Moreover, Arthur's promise was hollow. The Shinigami plot would be carried out while she was locked in her cell. Six months or six years, it didn't matter. Unless she was free, she would have no chance to save the city.

Kasey slowly stood up, stretching for the first time in hours. She straightened up to her full height.

Looking Arthur in the eye, she shook her head. "Not a chance."

Arthur grabbed the steel bars, his knuckles turning white. "Do you think you can deny me? Remember what happened when you tried to peer inside my mind, Kasey? I cast you out like a child. I could have melted your mind for your insolence. You are but a child playing at being an adult. What do you think will happen when I try to take what I want by force? I've done it before, and I'll do it again. Serial killers, sociopaths, terrorists. We have interrogated many over the years. Dangerous witches and wizards bent on the destruction of our community. They always try to resist but, in the end, we get what we want from them. The real question is, will there be anything left of your mind when I do?"

Kasey almost admired the Shinigami's act. She had to remind herself he wasn't Arthur. Clearly the role had become second nature to him by now.

It was no idle threat, though, and she knew it. But this time she was ready. If the Master of the Shinigami wanted inside her mind, she would fight him for it. She doubted he had encountered many prescient witches in his time and her mind was far from ordinary. If he tried to invade her thoughts, he'd get more than he bargained for.

Still, he would try. That much was certain. He'd come too far and paid too high a price to give up now. He wouldn't stop until he had Sanders. Kasey would have to decide: Sanders' life or her freedom.

Of course, it wasn't really much of a choice. Six months in jail meant she would still be in this hole when the city was destroyed. Doubtless this was the Master of the Shinigami's intention, but Kasey couldn't let on that she knew his identity. It wasn't in her nature to sacrifice someone she cared about.

No, she had to keep him talking to buy as much time as possible. "How did you know I would be in Central Park?"

Arthur laughed. "Oh, I saw the big googly eyes you and John were making at each other over dinner. His concern over you in the Administorum was admirable. Under different circumstances, I'm sure you two might have been very happy together. Classic love story. Boy meets girl. Boy falls in love with girl. Girl breaks three of his ribs and runs off with a murderer. Truly heartwarming. No, Kasey. I knew you would call him eventually, so we tapped his phone and waited. You walked right into our trap. You never stood a chance."

Kasey ground her teeth. She wanted nothing more than to punch him in his smug face.

"That's what you don't get, Kasey. You are just two renegades. I have the entire might of the Arcane Council. I can grind you into the dust."

"Grind away," Kasey replied. "If you kill me, you'll have no idea where Sanders is, and with that much money, you will never find him. What time is it, by the way? I'm not really sure how long I was out. He might already be gone."

"Enough. If you won't see reason, I'll have to take matters into my own hands. We tried the carrot. I guess we'll have to try the stick."

Kasey fought to keep the smile from her face as a plan formed in her mind.

"I guess I should have expected this from you, you stubborn little wretch." Arthur waved his hand across cages lock and chanted, "*Onlucan.*"

At his arcane instruction, the lock rolled back into place. Arthur strode into the cell.

Looming over Kasey, he looked her in the eye. "I did warn you, Miss Chase, but you wouldn't listen. Now you can have it your way."

He reached out his hand and placed it on Kasey's forehead.

She closed her eyes and cleared her mind. Focusing all of her energy, she sought for the silence inside of her. She sought the essence at the center of her being. The inner sanctum of her mind where her prescience resided.

Words flowed off Arthur's tongue, the baritone chant reverberating through the cell. Kasey paid it no heed. However, as she felt the intrusion into her mind, she doubled her resolve.

As Arthur attempted to beat down her defenses, Kasey took a different approach. Drawing on the power of her mind, she called forth her gifts.

*Arthur wants a story, so let's tell him one.*

Kasey reveled as she felt her power well up inside her. Opening her eyes, she felt the familiar mist descending. As she did so, she took the last option Arthur would expect: she lowered her defenses and let him in.

The mist lifted and Kasey found herself standing on a busy New York street. Traffic ambled by in both directions, angry commuters using their horns liberally. In New York City, impatience was always in oversupply.

Kasey looked up. Here in downtown Manhattan, she was surrounded on every side by immense skyscrapers. If she had a clear line of sight, she would have been able to see the Empire State building a stone's throw away.

The street was one she knew all too well—Lexington Avenue. She had traveled it many times. She stood outside one of New York's iconic structures. The Waldorf Astoria was a legend in the New York hotel game. With a history stretching back decades, it had earned its place in the New York City skyline.

Kasey glanced about. Although she couldn't see Arthur, she had no doubt that the Master of the Shinigami could see all that she could see.

What he did not know was that the spectacle before him was a fabrication of Kasey's mind. Using her gifts, she was cobbling together a vision melded from memories from her past, mixed with her imagination. If this Shinigami was prescient, he might have been wary.

Gifted wizard that he was, his arrogance would be his undoing. Akihiro was not prescient, and without experience in seeing visions he would not recognize the tell-tale signs of Kasey's fabrication. The slightest blurring at her periphery, or in the places where memory met imagination. It was so subtle that the untrained eye would gloss straight over it. Kasey did her best not to draw undue attention to them. Her plan hinged on the Shinigami believing he had successfully gained entrance to her mind.

*You are in my playground now.*

Kasey glanced up at the Waldorf Astoria's sign and then pushed open the heavy glass door. She remembered the hotel well.

She had been a guest of the hotel for a medical examiner's conference. With the conference starting early and finishing late most evenings, she hadn't wanted to bother with the daily commute. She'd treated herself to a few nights in the luxurious Astoria and tremendously enjoyed the experience.

The hotel was just as she'd remembered. Its rich period furniture seemed straight out of the thirties.

She strode confidently across the lobby, past reception to the bank of elevators. She punched the button and the doors parted. After stepping onto the elevator, she tapped her foot as the door shut.

The elevator hurtled up to the fifteenth floor. As the elevator slowed to a halt, Kasey waited for the doors to part. A Japanese man in a suit was waiting to step onto the elevator.

Kasey made her way out of the elevator and wandered down the hall, counting the rooms as she went. The more time she took, the more time she bought. She couldn't appear too eager. Otherwise, the Master of the Shinigami might recognize her ploy. Reaching the door to 1505, Kasey fished around in her pocket and pulled out a key card. She hovered her hand by the door.

A voice inside her mind urged her onward. "Go inside, now."

*Oh, Arthur, your impatience is so predictable.*

Kasey slid the key card into the lock and the door opened. Pushing the heavy hotel door in, she stepped into the room. The small suite was dominated by two queen size beds. Laid out across each of the beds was row upon row of assault rifles. Dozens of spare clips and magazines lay in a pile at the end of the bed. Half a dozen handguns were sitting on the dresser, and on the coffee table rested a M249 fully automatic belt fed machine gun.

Kasey smiled at her imagination. It was enough firepower to fight a small war and would certainly be enough to get Arthur's attention. Sanders sat on the end of the bed, checking one of the assault rifles.

"Hey, Kasey! There you are. You had me worried sick. I thought that the ADI might've caught up with you."

Kasey laughed. "No, those clowns are days behind us. They're still investigating the attack on the Night Crew's stash house. They have no idea just how good a use we have put that money to."

Sanders grinned. "I'll say. Did you see that arms dealer's face when you opened the duffel full of cash? I thought his eyes were going to roll out of his head. He couldn't give us the guns quick enough."

Kasey sat down in the recliner. "Yeah, tell me about it. I imagine he would have sung a different tune if he knew just whose money it was."

"I'm sure he'll be less than impressed if the Night Crew manage to catch up with him. Shame he won't have any of these guns—they might have come in handy."

"Yup. Definitely two birds with one stone," Kasey replied. "Not only have we got these dangerous guns off the street, but we've also got enough firepower to take the fight to the Council. No more of this oppressive nonsense. It's time that we unseat Arthur Ainsley once and for all. How did you go on your recruiting drive?"

Sanders set down the gun. "Better than my wildest dreams. I knew that there were a lot of disaffected witches and wizards looking to take a swing at the council, but I guess with all my years spent working there, I just wanted to believe that the community had a better perception of us. After all, we were just trying to help keep them safe.

"Well, it turns out, there are more than a few witches and wizards ready to settle the score with the Chancellor. I used my case files from the last decade to identify who had the biggest axes to grind. Started with those who have recently been released from custody and worked my way back. Not all of them were happy to see me at first, but once I told them of our target, they were more than willing to lend a hand."

"How many did you get?" Kasey asked.

"All told, I think we'll get at least twenty," Sanders replied.

Kasey punched the air. "Fantastic. I got another six, so we are on our way to thirty. I thought we had enough firepower, but we may have to top up our supplies. You think there'll be enough to get the job done?"

Sanders surveyed the room. There were guns strewn on every surface. "I think so. Last they saw us, we were fleeing before them. They may have fortified their position at the Arcane Council, but they are just agents with pistols. What can they hope to do against an army of wizards armed to the teeth with assault rifles? One decisive strike, and we will cut the heart out of the Arcane Council. With Arthur gone, we will be able to move on with our life. It won't be long before the memory of Arthur fades. As it does, their will to hunt for us will too. We've still got more than enough cash, so we can disappear overseas and never be found. Once the Council has been dealt with, we will be free to live without having to look over our shoulder every day."

"So, when are we doing this?" Kasey asked.

Sanders picked up and checked one of the pistols. As he handed it to Kasey, his eyes narrowed. "Soon, Kasey, very soon."

*That ought to do.*

Closing her eyes, Kasey dispelled her vision. The manacles may have inhibited her ability to cast spells, but inside her mind she still reigned supreme.

With iron will, she slammed shut the steel gates of her mind, expelling Arthur unceremoniously with the same savagery he'd employed against her.

With their minds linked, Kasey lashed out psychically, doing her best to destroy Arthur's mind, but the ancient wizard was already prepared, dispelling her attempt with ease.

Releasing his hands, he tutted. "None of that, Kasey. An attempt on my life is not going to play well for you in court. Not that it really matters. I think we have everything we need. I did tell you, Kasey, we get what we want eventually. You would be wise not to resist."

"He will kill you; you know that Arthur. I've never seen anyone so determined," Kasey said.

"Determined he might be. Unfortunately for him, we know where he is and will crush him like the rodent that he is." Arthur turned and shouted into the darkness, "Ready the ADI! We have

Sanders' location. We'll need a hundred agents in tactical gear, ready to roll out immediately. I want no mistakes this time. We'll have Noah Sanders in a body bag by nightfall."

A storm of footsteps trailed off into the dark.

Kasey had to fight to keep from smiling. The Chancellor had fallen straight into her trap. She only wished she could get a warning to Sanders, so that he might make the most of the opportunity. In any event, she would succeed in wasting most of their afternoon.

Every minute mattered. If she was lucky, Sanders would be watching the Council for news of her and her capture. If Ainsley was foolish enough to join the sting, Sanders might get to take a shot at Ainsley himself.

As Arthur departed the cell, he slid the door shut and breathed an incantation to lock the cell door.

"You know, Kasey, I really do enjoy our chats. No matter how rebellious you seem at first, you always tend to come around and give me what I want eventually. It's one of your better qualities. Is there anything you want to tell me before I have you executed for treason?"

"Rot in hell," Kasey snarled, eager to sell her ploy.

"I'll be sure to tell Sanders the same," Arthur replied with a chuckle as he disappeared into the dark.

When the footsteps retreated, Kasey was alone once more. Now with time on her side, she set about making a real plan.

# CHAPTER 16

Kasey let out a heavy sigh as she lay exhausted on the stone floor of her cell. In the hours she had been left alone, she tried every conceivable spell, enchantment, and incantation. She had worn herself out trying to blast her way free. When her arcane efforts had failed her, she attempted to grind away at the cuffs or break them outright by beating them against the steel bars or the sparse furniture in her cell. All Kasey had to show for her efforts was a pair of chafed wrists.

Though the wrought iron shackles looked old and worn, they seemed as strong as the day they were first forged.

Kasey got the distinct impression that was more to do with the underlying enchantment than the materials themselves. Whatever spell that had brought them into being had also augmented their durability.

"I don't know what I was expecting," Kasey mumbled to herself.

There was no way she was the first witch to inhabit these cells. The realization dawned painfully. As long as she was wearing the cuffs, she was stuck down here.

Which brought her to her second problem: she didn't rightly know where *down here* was. From her conversation, she suspected that she was somewhere in the Arcane Council's headquarters. The vast underground metropolis stretched for miles. It made sense that the Arcane Council would lock up the worst of its felons in its most secure location. The proximity to the Council's Court would provide protection during the transfer of criminals as their cases were tried.

She was unsure what security measures would be in place beyond the cell. Doubtless there would be both magical and mundane lines of defenses. The vast chasm between where she was and what she needed to know in order to escape was too much for her to deal with.

If she was to get out of here in one piece, she was going to require assistance. Sanders would know of her capture by now. The ADI would have broadcasted their win far and wide. She wondered if her mother might come. Surely, she was entitled to some sort of legal representation. Could the ADI hold her without cause? Would she have an opportunity to defend herself at all?

She was in uncharted waters. She resigned herself to her fate. For the first time in days, her world was truly silent. In spite of her terrible predicament, she was grateful for the peace. She had grown weary of life on the run, and while being caught presented its own perils, the solitude of the cells was a welcome reprieve from the perpetual harrying of the ADI.

*Perhaps I might even get some sleep.*

Rolling over, Kasey wedged her hands underneath her face and attempted to doze off on her side. As her tired eyelids slowly descended, a door in the distance slammed open. The racket reverberated through the expanse, and Kasey began to get a feel for just how vast a chamber she was housed in.

Arthur Ainsley approached her cell, the veins in his neck threatening to explode at any moment.

Kasey sat up. "Well, Chancellor, so good to see you. How was your little excursion?"

The scarlet coloring in Arthur's cheeks was growing brighter and brighter by the moment. His rage was almost luminous.

"You lied to us," he said with a snarl. "You sent us on a wild goose chase."

Kasey placed a hand on her chest innocently. "Why, me? I would never do such a thing. After all, I didn't tell you anything. You took your answers out of my mind of your own free will. I can't help if you're ignorant or uninformed when it comes to a superior mind. How is the Astoria this time of year? I suppose it's beautiful."

Arthur grasped the bars. "My agents just spent hours tearing the hotel apart. He was nowhere to be seen."

"I expect not," Kasey replied, scratching at the nape of her neck. "We've never even been to the Astoria. Not together, anyway. I went years ago, and it was lovely. I'm not really sure why you expected him to be there. I guess that's what you get for poking around in other people's minds."

"You insolent little witch! You think you can toy with me? I am the Chancellor of the Arcane Council. I was willing to be lenient if you would give us Sanders, but if you're too stupid to see the wisdom in that course of action, then we'll be forced to use more invasive methods."

Kasey placed her hands in her lap. "Torture? Or are you going to read my mind again? How did that go for you last time? You want to be careful, Arthur. You don't even know what I'm capable of. If you come to play in my mind again, you might just get lost in there. I might be a little child, but you are an ignorant old fool."

Arthur shook the cell bars. After several deep breaths he looked Kasey in the eye and replied. "Oh, no, I shan't bother reading your mind again, Kasey. This time we'll try a different approach. If we can't find Sanders, we will make him come to us. Even unwilling, I am sure you will prove just as useful as bait. If Sanders gives a damn about you, he'll have to come out of his hole."

"Good luck with that. I doubt he's still in the country," Kasey said.

"Oh, he's here," Arthur said. "That poor fool doesn't know when to let things go. He'll still be working the Getz case, trying tirelessly to clear his name. When he hears word of your trial, I'm sure he'll pay us a visit. If not for your trial, then certainly for your execution."

"Execution?" Kasey stammered, as Arthur's declaration cut her to the core. "You have no grounds."

Arthur smiled. "Oh, no, Miss Chase, that is where you are mistaken. In the last two weeks alone, you've showed reckless disregard for our laws. You have broken into the Arcane Council, you've attacked our agents on numerous occasions. We have footage of you and Sanders laying waste not only to our people but setting fire to the building doing untold millions of dollars' worth of damage. Not to mention the priceless damage you did in the archives. Some of those records will never be recovered. Don't even get me started on the evidence you destroyed. Oh, yes, we know why you went to the evidence locker. Doubtless trying to conceal your attempt to kidnap me."

"Kidnap?" Kasey asked, concerned that Arthur might be too close to the truth. "We should have killed you while we had the chance."

"Yes, I thought that was you in the church. No one else is quite as brazenly foolish as you are, Miss Chase. You see, I don't need to fabricate a case against you. You have been working tirelessly night and day as long as I've known you to build a case against yourself. While you served a purpose, I was willing to stay justice on your behalf. But now that you've aligned yourself with Sanders, all I really need to do is get out of the way and let justice take its toll. I have no doubt how the Council will vote. Your display the other week certainly poisoned most of them against you. Even Sanders didn't enjoy your visit. I think your trial will be the fastest capital trial the Council has ever seen."

Kasey was speechless. She wanted to fight back, but she could see the futility of it. Everything Arthur had said was true, albeit out of context. She had done all those things. She had done the wrong thing but for the right reason.

Unfortunately, without Getz's killer in custody, she seemed destined to be on the wrong side of the truth.

Her only hope now rested on revealing Arthur as the Master of the Shinigami, but she needed witnesses and lots of them. She needed everyone to know the truth. Her best chance lay before her; as a high profile criminal, her trial would be well attended.

"You see, Kasey, you know it's true," Arthur continued. "There is plenty of footage of your assaulting agents, and detailed records of your using your magic repeatedly in front of normals. No one in recent times has done more to endanger our world than you. It's a fitting cause for an execution if ever there was one. I'll simply have our media outlets broadcast the truth: The infamous criminal Kasey Chase is in ADI custody, about to stand trial for her crimes. Arcane Council in disbelief at the magnitude of her transgressions. Chancellor seeks the death penalty. I think that'll get Sanders' attention. What do you think, Kasey?"

"I think you're going to get exactly what you deserve," she said, trying her best to put on a brave face, while her heart raced inside her. "And sooner rather than later."

"Oh, that's cute. You think Sanders will be your knight in shining armor? I doubt it. Your insolence is at its end. Enjoy the last few hours of your life, Kasey, because that's all that remains. The trial begins tomorrow morning at eight. Get some sleep, because you are going to want to be wide awake for that. The Council will appoint a defense counsel for you. Not that it will do you any good."

"Don't bother." Kasey replied. "I'll represent myself."

Arthur scoffed. "Defiant until the end." He laughed as he walked away. Stopping, he looked over his shoulder, he added, "Any request for a last meal?"

Kasey thought about it for a moment.

Arthur laughed. "This isn't a movie, Kasey. You are going to die tomorrow. You hardly need a last meal."

With his laugh reverberating through the prison, Arthur disappeared into the darkness, leaving Kasey alone to contemplate her fate.

# CHAPTER 17

In the darkness of the cell, it was difficult to mark the passage of time. Kasey had never been one for wearing a watch but could have used one now. She had tried to rest as best she could, but the cold stone floor and iron shackles had made it an uncomfortable prospect.

Her looming fate hadn't helped her cause. Lying flat on her cell floor she ran over her plan again in her mind. A clanging at the door of the cell drew her attention. Kasey groaned as she opened her eye, expecting to see Arthur standing there once more.

Instead, it was a full detail, six ADI agents. At their lead was a blonde-haired agent with a strong jaw line. At any other time, Kasey might have considered him handsome. The stubble evident on his chin showed that it had been a long night for him also.

"What's all this, then?" Kasey asked. "All of you for just one girl? I feel flattered."

"You shouldn't," the leader replied. "The council is in session. You're about to have a front row seat to your own destruction. On the plus side, it's standing room only. I've never seen such a throng. We couldn't even fit everyone in the chambers. It appears you've become something of a celebrity, Miss Chase. It's a shame you won't be alive long enough to enjoy it."

The agent swept his hand over the lock issuing the arcane command, *"Onlucan."*

The cogs in the lock whirled into place and opened.

Grabbing the steel gate, he opened the gate and then nodded to his men. The other agents filed into the cell.

Cornered like a rat in a trap, Kasey stood her ground, staring them down.

"Miss Chase," the leader said, "I'd advise you not to compound your problems by adding another assault to your record. If you are willing to behave, we can remove the leg irons and leave them here. But if you force us to, we will truss you like a turkey and carry you into the chambers. Either way, you'll be brought before the court. It's really your choice on the manner of your arrival."

"I don't suppose I could get you to remove these as well?" Kasey asked, holding up her shackles toward the agents.

The leader laughed. "Nice try. I wasn't born yesterday."

Kasey sighed. "That's a shame. Would have given us a fresh start on your personality." She dropped her hands and nodded to the men. "Ready when you are, boys."

The agents closed in. One of them bent down and inserted a key into the shackles binding her feet. In one deft motion, he unlocked the shackles along with the chain that had kept Kasey tethered to the center of the cell. Now only the cuffs and the agents stood between her and freedom.

Every bone in her body told her to be defiant but shackled and outnumbered six to one in the tiny cell, even Kasey didn't fancy her prospects.

Now it seemed she would get her day in court after all—whether she wanted it or not.

One agent stood on either side of her as they escorted her out of her prison. Then, with Blondie McJawline and another agent running point, an agent at each side, and two bringing up the rear, she made her way through the cells.

The party walked past row after row of cells, eventually reaching a large steel door. The door was open, and the party proceeded through it into a hallway. The trailing agent sealed the steel door shut behind them.

The hallway was only slightly more furnished than her cell had been. It had tiles instead of the cobblestone floor, cheap wallpaper and a faded blue carpet runner that ran the length of the hallway.

The party trudged along the hall for what seemed like an eternity.

Kasey busily scanned the corridor looking for any opportunity to escape. The agents kept a close eye on her, their hands never far from their weapons and their eyes watching her every movement. No doubt the Chancellor had been explicit in his directions. If there was going to be a chance to break out, she would have to manufacture it herself.

Kasey did her best to measure the distance from the cells to the Council Chamber to try and gauge the location of the prison, but distracted by the agents surrounding her, she soon lost count.

The party arrived at a set of hardwood stairs. The tacky wallpaper that had lined the corridor gave way to wood paneling. Kasey recognized the style from her earlier visit to the Council Chambers. She knew they were nearing the end of her journey. No doubt, the stairs would take them before the Council and the assembled court.

The party started up the stairs. Kasey was on the fourth step when the agent beside her slipped. He knocked into her as he fell on his face. She stumbled back, flailing for a handhold. Her back slammed into someone. She toppled down the stairs, landing in a heap with two other agents.

Kasey did her best to extricate herself from the mess but with the cuffs it was difficult to untangle herself. The agent behind her wrestled himself free. An older agent with a thick salt-and-pepper beard reached down and scooped Kasey up. He set her on her feet, then looked down and checked her cuffs. As he did so, she felt something pressed into the palm of her hand. The agent's hand clasped shut around her own.

She looked up at the agent who gave her the faintest smile before winking at her. The motion was so quick Kasey wondered if she had seen it at all. A second later the smile faded.

"On your feet now, Chase," he snapped. "We'll not have any more of that tomfoolery from you. Another stunt like that and the Chancellor will have your head."

Kasey nodded along and dropped her hands. The last thing she wanted was for the agents' suspicions to be aroused. The agents collected themselves and escorted her up the stairs.

At the top of the stairs was a heavy oak door. The lead agent opened the door to reveal the Council Chambers Kasey had visited only weeks before.

As Kasey was escorted into the hall, the audience erupted. Hurried whisperings broke out in the gallery as the crowd strained their necks to get a better look at her.

She looked at the roof. It seemed the damage that had been done in their previous escape had since been repaired.

She entered the courtroom, searching the swarm of assembled spectators for a familiar face. The crowd whispered and jeered. It seemed from the spirit in the room that Kasey's fate was a foregone conclusion. Those gathered were eager to watch a verdict be handed down and enjoy the temporary pleasure to be had watching another's misfortune unfold.

Then in the midst of everything, a face she knew all too well. Front and center behind the defendant's desk was her mother. She stood there with an expression that could have been carved from stone.

As Kasey's eyes locked on to hers, she caught a glimmer in her mother's eye that threatened to roll down her cheek. Jane's hands gripped the wooden balustrade before her until her knuckles turned white.

Kasey had never seen her mother so distraught. The ADI cordon guided Kasey through the room and sat her at the desk. She slid her chair forward until she was safely ensconced behind the table. The ADI departed and took up their posts around the chamber.

Shielded by the table, Kasey took a moment to look down and check on the object that had been pressed into her hand.

It was a key.

Clenching her fist shut, she studied the agent that had given it to her. He, along with another agent, stood below the council's raised lectern. The agent nodded slowly. For the first time in two days, Kasey had hope.

Above the agent, the Arcane Council sat behind their raised bench, forcing the occupants of the court to look up in order to see them. Kasey tried to get a read on them, but their faces were impassive. Everyone except for the Shinigami masquerading as Arthur Ainsley; he looked positively jubilant.

*Note to self, he needs a punch in his smug face.*

Blondie McJawline raised his hand for silence. When the courtroom didn't respond, he shouted over the din, "Silence! This session of the Arcane Council is called to order. Please, be seated."

The assembled masses took their seats and Kasey braced herself.

With the courtroom silent at last, he continued. "As you well know, Kasey Chase was recently apprehended by the ADI. The list of charges levied against her by the council is substantial. Prosecutor, if you'd be so kind as to read them for us, so that the court might understand the gravity of the charges being considered today."

Kasey glanced to her left, to the table that housed the chief prosecutor. The man wore a simple pinstripe suit, and his jet black hair was slicked back. The corners of his mouth edged upward. Clearly, he was excited for his day in court.

Kasey hated him immediately.

The prosecutor stood, buttoned his suit, and then lifted a file off the table. Strutting out from behind his desk, he addressed the Council.

"Witches and wizards of the Council, the case against Miss Chase is extensive. Her utter disrespect for the law is matched only by her disregard for human life. The charges against her are as follows. Two counts of break and entry. One count of theft." The prosecutor paused and eyed the room before adding, "That we know of. Thirty-four counts of damaging Council property with damages totaling in excess of five million dollars. Tampering with evidence, obstructing an ongoing investigation. Ninety-six counts of assaulting an agent. Widespread vandalizing and damage throughout the city, including attacking and defacing the priceless Lady of Liberty. Aiding and abetting a felon, in particular the notable ex-director of the ADI and the man responsible for the murder of Theodore Getz." The prosecutor finished with a flourish.

The court erupted into a furor of whispers and muttering.

Arthur Ainsley raised his hand for silence. "Silence! We will have silence in the court, or we will eject the gallery from the proceedings."

The whispers died down.

Arthur continued. "Miss Chase, the charges against you are extensive. The council has recommended that you obtain legal counsel, which suggestion you have rejected entirely. Before we proceed, you must understand that lack of adequate counsel will not prove sufficient grounds for a mistrial. If you proceed unrepresented, our verdict here today will stand, and you will bear the full consequences of your actions. Do you understand me?"

"I do," Kasey replied, her heart pounding.

Another member of the Council, an elderly woman, leaned over the lectern. "Very well, Miss Chase. How do you plead?"

Kasey leaned forward until her mouth was mere inches from the microphone. "Not guilty."

# CHAPTER 18

The courtroom exploded into a frenzy. The witches and wizards in the gallery protested Kasey's flagrant flaunting of the court.

"Order! Order in the court!" Arthur rose to his feet. "We will have silence, or the gallery will be ejected. This is your final warning."

As the gallery quietened down, Arthur's gaze narrowed on Kasey.

"Miss Chase," he said, "I fear I must have misheard you. Could we have your plea again? Thank you."

Kasey leaned forward and tapped the microphone. The dull thud echoed through the room. "Oh, it is working. It must just be you, Chancellor. The plea was *not guilty* and your threat to empty the gallery twice before we've even begun in earnest has me wondering. Why are you so anxious to conduct the proceedings of this particular trial without an audience?"

"Because it's a courtroom, not a circus, Miss Chase. I will not have you making a mockery of our justice system."

Kasey grinned. "I wouldn't dare. Besides, the noise being produced by the gallery could scarcely be attributed to my disrespect for your criminal justice system. I think you are merely afraid of how you will look in the court of public opinion. After all, the Chancellor serves at the will of the people, does he not?"

"That's enough! It's you who is on trial, Kasey, not me."

Kasey nodded. "I'm aware of that, Chancellor. You have my plea and I maintain my position. Not guilty on all counts."

The counselor beside Arthur, an august woman of advancing years, pulled the microphone away from him and toward herself. "Miss Chase, my name is Alice Hoskins. You are aware that we have video footage of many of these crimes being committed. There is little doubt in the council's mind that you are the person in the footage. Might I ask on what grounds you could possibly contend that you are not guilty? Or, as the Chancellor has asserted, are you merely trying to make a mockery of this courtroom?"

Kasey had her audience and she was ready to perform for them. "That's an excellent question, Councilwoman, one that lies at the very heart of what I feel we truly need to discuss today. The grounds on which I make my claim are simple. The lesser charges we could deal with one by one, but first if I might speak to the more serious allegations against me, I would offer my defense that at the times in question, I was not acting as a private citizen contravening the laws of the Arcane Council. I had, in fact, been deputized by then Director Sanders to conduct those activities, which he had sanctioned. In many instances, we were opposed by other agents of the ADI who had been subverted by the Chancellor to act on his behalf and further his interests, but never at any time to date have I taken action contrary to what Director Sanders had instructed me to do."

The prosecutor scoffed. "Objection, your honors. Director Sanders stands accused of the murder of Theodore Getz. As a result of which, he was removed from office by the Chancellor and is currently being hunted by this Council and its agents. Unfortunately, he remains at large and so cannot be here to answer for his own crimes. Neither can he corroborate this outlandish claim. Miss Chase's ridiculous defense rests on a fallacy and fiction that we simply can't entertain."

Councilwoman Hoskins slid down her glasses and looked at Kasey over their wire rims. "Miss Chase, the prosecutor has a point."

The prosecutor sat down, a grin crossing his face.

"Oh, he would, your honor, if any of it were true. It is correct that Director Sanders is currently being pursued by the ADI. But he is being pursued for a murder he did not commit and for which he has not yet been tried nor convicted. Therefore, I move that he remains innocent until proven guilty by this court, and assert that I was, in fact, acting under his rightful direction to help bring the true murderer of Theodore Getz to justice—a pursuit and duty of his office that he continues to carry out to this day, in spite of his recent, unlawful, and baseless removal from office. So, as I have said, the only actions I took against agents of the ADI were to contend with those acting under the usurped authority of Chancellor Ainsley. The allegations that I broke into this building are inaccurate. I contend that I walked in through the front door, escorted by the Director himself."

The prosecutor was on his feet in a heartbeat. "Using an illegal illusion spell, designed to imitate agents of the ADI—a serious charge in and of itself."

A balding Councilman on the far left of the platform waved his hand. "Sit down, Mr. Prosecutor. You'll have your chance. Now, let Miss Chase finish so we can move on."

The prosecutor slumped into his seat and folded his arms.

Kasey continued. "It was an illusion that was cast not by myself, but by the director, not only to protect ourselves from harm but also to protect agents of the ADI acting under the wrongful influence of the Chancellor. It was Director Sanders' greatest desire to preserve and protect the lives of his agents, irrespective of whose commands they were currently following. The illusion was a means for us to carry out our mission without causing undue harm to come to the Council or any of its agents."

Arthur chortled. "For all the good it did. You landed dozens of agents in the Administorum and caused millions of dollars of damage to this facility. Damage that we have video footage of you committing. You also broke into the evidence lockup and tampered with evidence surrounding the Getz's case."

"That's a lie," Kasey said, clenching her fists. "We did enter the evidence lockup, that much is correct. But we both know the only piece of evidence we touched pertained to a scuffle that took place in St. Patrick's Cathedral earlier that day."

Arthur smiled triumphantly. "I wonder why you would have tampered with that particular evidence? Could it be that you and Director Sanders were behind the attack on my life in the cathedral? An attack that left an elderly priest unconscious. One that could have killed him? An innocent normal and a pillar of the community. We haven't even begun to draft charges for those actions, Miss Chase, but at your admission we can happily have them added to the docket."

"I will not perjure myself," Kasey said. "It was me in the church. The attack the Chancellor is asserting did in fact take place, but at no point in time was there any attempt against his life. The Chancellor himself was incapacitated. Had we harbored him any ill will, we could have killed him there and then. It was in fact the elderly priest we were concerned with. We worried that someone may have stolen his identity in order to attack the Chancellor. We believed it to be the same person who had perpetrated the murder of Theodore Getz. The attack was in fact an attempt to save the Chancellor's life. One for which we have never, ever been thanked."

The courtroom's gallery broke into frenzied murmurs.

"The only danger I was in that day was from you and the director," Ainsley countered. "I'll not thank you for staging an elaborate ruse. And my comments regarding my dear friend, the Archbishop, stand."

"Indeed, they might," Kasey said, "but the attack you refer to utilized tear gas against a normal. I'm an agent of the New York Police Department. I was employing police resources in the furtherance of an ongoing investigation. Any issues the Archbishop has can be dealt with in the courts of the land. We have no need to waste the council's time with these trivial side quests."

Councilwoman Hoskins interjected. "While they may pale compared to some of the crimes of which you stand accused, be assured, Miss Chase, we consider them each a serious offense. The Council will not have its laws flaunted. While we've given you latitude to explain your bizarre and unbelievable plea, it rests with us to determine the merit of it. Having entered your plea, I hand the time over to the prosecution to make its case. Miss Chase, in the interests of time, I will instruct you not to interrupt the prosecutor's remarks. You will have ample opportunity to make your own case at the conclusion of his remarks, before any verdict is reached and any sentence is handed down. Do you understand me?"

"I do, your honor." Kasey leaned back in her chair. "This ought to be good."

The prosecutor stood, adjusted his suit, and rounded the table. Strutting back and forth before the council's lectern like a peacock, he addressed them. "Our venerable council. As Miss Chase has so rightly declared, the judgment for many of the actions she has committed hinge on the guilt or innocence of Noah Sanders. It seems difficult, if not impossible, to accurately decide her fate while the case against the Director remains incomplete. Now, I believe this is an elaborate ruse prepared by the defendant to forestall the hand of justice. We have on excellent authority that Miss Chase and Mr. Sanders conducted an unsanctioned raid of a criminal organization during which they made off with a substantial sum of money. With the millions they have illegally obtained, Mr. Sanders has not only his prodigious arcane talent but these immense resources at his disposal. He can ensure that he evades the authority of this council almost indefinitely. As we cannot conduct a case against one who is not, and may never be, present, I feel it necessary to raise the evidence against Mr. Sanders here, so that the members of the Council might view Miss Chase's actions in the proper light. That is, someone acting under the influence and directions of a murderer, not a vigilante hero as she has so eloquently asserted."

Kasey bit her lip. With every fiber of her being, she wanted nothing more than to leap the table and punch him in his smug mouth. He was a gifted lawyer—she had to give him that—but if she'd been given five minutes alone in a room with him, she had no doubt there would be little left but a pile of broken bones.

She took a deep breath to suppress her rising rage.

The prosecutor walked back to his table, opened his case and pulled out a file. "I would present to the court exhibit A—a ballistics report taken from the slugs that ended poor Theodore Getz's life. Ballistics on the weapon in question were a precise match to the service weapon of Noah Sanders. Sanders' own gun was the instrument of Getz's death, a weapon that was never reported missing and has not been seen since. Second, video evidence of Sanders entering the building, dragging an unconscious Mr. Getz in a wheelchair. It was in the basement of this very building in which Mr. Getz was found the next morning, having been brutally tortured and murdered. It is very well that

Mr. Sanders is not here today. Frankly, the case against him is as watertight as a mermaid's brassiere."

The court broke out into laughter.

"With these entered into evidence, it is the opinion of the prosecution that Miss Chase has not only sought to muddy the waters and destroy evidence, but that she has acted as an accomplice after the fact to help Director Sanders escape justice. They are the grounds on which she is being tried. These other charges, many of which are serious crimes, carry considerable sentences in their own right. She is as guilty of each of those as Sanders is of murder. The fact that she appears to have been swayed by some bizarre Stockholm syndrome is no defense for these unconscionable acts. It is merely a mitigating circumstance that the council in their wisdom and mercy might consider at sentencing."

He strolled back to his suitcase and produced a stack of manila folders. He dropped them on the desk. "I enter as exhibits three through thirty-five, sworn testimonies of the agents she attacked, all of whom spent time in the Administorum as a result of Miss Chase's actions. As Exhibit thirty-six through forty-five, we have video surveillance footage of Miss Chase recklessly using her magic in public places, placing our world at risk of discovery and our community in danger of reprisal from the normal population of New York. If this is not enough, I would tender as Exhibit forty-six the repair bill for the damage done to the very structure in which we sit, a structure that if it wasn't for the tireless efforts of our emergency personnel may have been wholly destroyed by the fire she helped set."

Raising his hand, he railed on. "The damages are in the millions, the damage done in the archives has been irreparable. The prosecution is pushing for the maximum sentence for this unhinged and dangerous individual. For her crimes against the agency and damage caused to the council, we would have pushed for life imprisonment. Unfortunately, Miss Chase is too dangerous and unhinged an individual to contain and has proved herself adept and capable of causing destruction in almost any circumstance. As a result, and in consideration of the ongoing danger she poses to our community, we push that Miss Chase should be executed for her crimes."

The prosecutor took his seat as the courtroom devolved into chatter.

Kasey watched as Arthur's smile spread.

The devious old cretin was actually enjoying this. Kasey clenched her fists and forced herself to draw in and exhale a deep breath. Her fists were so tight she felt the key cutting into the palm of her hand.

Councilwoman Hoskins raised a hand to quiet the courtroom. "Miss Chase. The court will now hear your defense. Take all the time you need. We remind you of the gravity of your crimes and the extent of the punishment that the prosecution is seeking. With that in mind, the floor is yours."

Kasey raised her handcuffs up so that they rested just beneath the table, an angle that would be impossible for any of the council members to see what she was up to. Deftly, she slid the key into the lock and turned it. The cuffs loosened.

Looking up at the council, she said, "Your honors. Ladies and gentlemen of the Arcane Council and those witnessing today's events. Our prosecutor has been so good as to make the bulk of my case for me and so I have only a little more to add to it. It would seem that the entirety of his comments hinge not on my guilt or innocence but rather on Director Sanders, who has been wrongfully accused and maligned in this court here today. I wish he was able to be here to defend himself. But as he isn't, I will happily do so in his stead. Only two weeks ago, I was summoned before the council to give an accounting of my actions. I was frank and direct then, and have no other intention today. I made clear then that the true threat was not any of my actions but was in fact an imminent attack against New York City being orchestrated by a foreign and dangerous power bent on our destruction."

"Not this again, Miss Chase." Arthur declared loudly. "You'll not muddy the waters here today with your conspiracy theories and nonsense."

Kasey ignored Arthur, instead addressing the other members of the council. "Men and women of the council, I believe I was given leave to defend myself. Given the seriousness of the accusations against me and the severity of the punishment been sought by the prosecution, I had expected to be able to at least finish my opening statements before being waylaid by the prosecution or the Chancellor. It doesn't say much for your impartiality if I can be attacked by the Chairman of this very body while offering my own defense."

Councilwoman Hoskins nodded. "Very well, Miss Chase. You may continue. The Chancellor will hold further comments until you are finished, but I warn you, you're on a short leash. If we determine that you are merely stalling or wasting the court's time with this nonsense, we'll hold you in contempt and add those charges and punishment to your sentence."

Kasey nodded. "Noted, your honor. Given the charges laid against me, I'm willing to chance it. After all, what is a fate worse than death itself?"

The court murmured and Kasey used the opportunity to click open her cuffs and slide the discarded shackles beneath her onto the chair. Free at last, she rubbed her chafing wrists.

As the murmuring died down, Kasey stood. Careful to keep her hands together before her, concealed by the sleeves of her jacket as not to arouse any suspicion, she walked around the table and into the aisle.

"As I was saying, the attack I warned of is now imminent. Events are proceeding quicker than we had hoped and while we are still struggling to identify the parties responsible, we are certain that their plan remains intact. It will deal catastrophic damage to New York City. Many of the events in recent weeks have been conducted toward this end. We believe that the death of Theodore Getz was yet another cog in their machinations."

"How utterly ridiculous," Arthur declared. "What possible evidence could you have that Theodore's murder has anything to do with this supposed attack on the city?"

"Chancellor, if you will give me a moment, I will tell you. That is my intention. In fact, it's why I'm here today."

"You are here today to answer the serious charges that have been leveled against you," Arthur barked.

Kasey smiled. "Of course... That, too."

She paced before the council. "As I was saying, and as the Chancellor is very well aware, I am prescient. I've been afflicted with visions of the future ever since I was a child. Sometimes I see a single person, other times, it's an entire group of people. It can be a horrendous thing to know someone's fate.

"For those of you less familiar with the gift, when I come into contact with people or places, I'm often granted a brief look into their life. Unfortunately, this often manifests with a heart-wrenching glimpse into one of the more terrifying experiences of their life. Often, it's a strong emotional event, like a birth or a death. I've often wished to be free of this burden, but to no avail.

"When I was twelve years old, my gift manifested and ever since I have been afflicted with the same vision of a city being laid waste. If you dig back into the records from my time at the academy, you will find evidence of them there. My gifts are well known and well documented. You will need to look under my birth name, though. You will find I changed it when I moved to New York City. My name is in fact Elizabeth Stonemoore. You will find that the Academy had me tested and discerned conclusively that my gifts were authentic and not the fevered imaginations of a child's mind."

Hopkins interrupted, "We can certainly investigate your assertions, Miss Stonemoore, but I still fail to see what relevance any of this holds for today's proceedings."

"If you will bear with me but a moment longer, Councilwoman, I shall make it painfully obvious." Kasey took a deep breath. "When Director Sanders and I infiltrated the council headquarters and the ADI, it was not to destroy evidence as you have supposed. Though I will admit that we did enter the evidence locker, our principal purpose was to deduce the identity of the murderer of Theodore Getz. We sought to clear the director's name and find the killer's true identity, so that we could bring him to justice. The director has and always will continue to pursue his mandate to defend the people of this great city. We broke into the morgue, so that I might bring myself into contact with Mr. Getz. My hope was that a vision would manifest and reveal to us Getz's true killer. We did, and it did. I stand here before you today to declare in no uncertain terms that Director Sanders was framed for a murder he did not commit."

"Well, if that's not the most convenient thing I've ever heard, Miss Chase," Arthur interjected. "You saw a vision that exonerates your accomplice."

"Chancellor, if you please," the balding councilman at the end of the lectern called. "Let her finish."

Chancellor Ainsley yielded reluctantly.

Kasey continued. "I also bring you incontrovertible evidence that Sanders is innocent. It is not convenient or a coincidence at all that I'm here today. Didn't you think that it was a little odd that after weeks of staying a step ahead of you, I just wandered haplessly into your trap in Central Park? Please, rest assured, Arthur, I'm exactly where I intended to be."

Kasey smiled as the Chancellor shifted uncomfortably in his seat. She might have been lying through her teeth but that mattered little now. It was time.

*It's all or nothing.*

The court dissolved into feverish murmuring. Kasey raised her hand for quiet.

The gesture didn't go unnoticed.

Ainsley's eyes locked onto her raised wrist. Before he could open his mouth, Kasey cut him off. "I would show the court that Theo's true killer is here in this very room today. It is no other than Chancellor Arthur Ainsley." Kasey swept her hand before her and chanted, "*Datguddiad.*"

The power swept out from Kasey's outstretched hand like a wave even as the ADI agents leapt toward her.

Arthur raised his hands and shouted, "This is outrageous."

The wave of power rolled over the Council as Kasey was tackled to the floor. Kasey's spell struck the Chancellor, driving away his illusion. As the spell dissipated, it revealed a Japanese man in his late forties. His hair was tied up in a ceremonial topknot. A simple silk robe was fastened by an ornamental sash at his waist.

It was Akihiro Igarashi, the Master of the Shinigami.

The courtroom went silent. Kasey could barely see through the pile of agents atop her.

She twisted to the side and shouted, "Or should I say, the Master of the Shinigami who killed Arthur Ainsley over a year ago so that he could infiltrate this council and perpetrate his plot against New York City. There's your killer, standing right before you."

Stunned silence descended on the courtroom.

# CHAPTER 19

The courtroom was deathly still as the Master of the Shinigami stood revealed at the center of the Arcane Council. Kasey struggled against the weight of the ADI pressing down on her. "Don't worry about me, you idiots. It's him you need to arrest."

Kasey locked eyes with the Master of the Shinigami. His cold gray eyes bored into hers. Contempt welled up in their depths. His ruse had come to a premature end.

He was murderous.

Before the ADI could process what had happened, the Master of the Shinigami reached down to his waist and drew the blade that rested there. In one swift motion, he brought it up and through the neck of the councilman seated to his right.

The councilman's head rolled off his shoulders, as the Shinigami turned to his left and shouted, "*Mahou no hari.*"

A beam of azure light bored through Councilwoman Hopkins. The gallery screamed.

From her place on the floor, Kasey struggled to see the extent of the damage being done, but she knew every second mattered. The Master of the Shinigami was laying waste to the Arcane Council. Several members retaliated but it was like trying to stop a hurricane with a handkerchief.

Kasey felt a weight being lifted off her back. Looking over her shoulder, she saw an agent being pulled away. Seconds later, another was unceremoniously ejected. The same bearded agent who had handed her the key earlier was now struggling to free her.

Kasey rolled onto her back and shoved the last of the agents off her. Pointing at Akihiro she shouted, "Get with the program, it's him you need to be concerned with."

The bearded agent reached down and extended his hand. Kasey took it and was yanked to her feet. She collided into his chest.

"Tell me that's you under there, Noah," she murmured.

"Sure is, Kasey. When I realized they had you, I had to improvise. I knew I'd not make it inside with another illusion. They were checking every visitor. So, I went old school." Noah ripped off the prosthetic mask and cast it aside.

Kasey stretched her cramped limbs. "It's good to see you. Thanks for the key, by the way. He didn't see that coming."

Sanders grinned. "No, he did not. But we still need to take him down before he escapes. He has bigger plans than killing us. He can't be allowed to leave."

The spectators in the gallery were running for their lives. The one exception was a woman in her fifties who was clambering over the wooden balustrade. Kasey did a double take.

It was her mother.

Her mother's eyes were fixed on the carnage taking place behind the Council's bench. At its center, the Master of the Shinigami was a symphony of destruction.

Her mother raised both hands and bellowed over the ruckus in the courtroom, "*Llusgo Hud.*"

A scarlet lance of pure arcane energy sliced through the courtroom toward the Master of the Shinigami. The bench itself provided no protection as the lance ripped straight through the wood work, showering the room in splinters. The lance hurtled toward the Shinigami.

Kasey's heart leapt as the lance bore down on their enemy. The beam struck him in the torso but rather than cut through him, it simply washed over the Master as a blossom of emerald energy played over him.

Kasey's hopes sank as the arcane energy dissipated harmlessly. The Shinigami appeared to have some sort of shield protecting him from harm.

The Shinigami turned on the courtroom. He smiled menacingly as he took in Kasey, her mother, and Sanders standing side-by-side defiantly.

"Director Sanders, nice of you to join us." The Shinigami glowered.

"I will be your end," Sanders replied.

The Shinigami sheathed his weapon. Then his head snapped up and he waved both hands in the air before him. *"Hi No Nami."*

A torrent of fire leapt from his outstretched hands.

Her mother wove a golden matrix of wards around the three of them.

The fire was deflected harmlessly, but the wards didn't protect the courtroom. The flames caught on the plush carpet and wooden furnishings.

Even as the fire rolled over them, a thunderbolt struck the center of the shield. The wards trembled under the onslaught but did not yield.

With both hands, Kasey summoned a wave of crushing kinetic energy. Even though the Shinigami was shielded, Kasey simply sought to level the playing field. Her blast struck the council bench. Kasey blew the already battered bench apart, leaving only a splintered ruin where it had once been. The Shinigami might have been shielded but his enchantment couldn't protect him from gravity. As the bench was blown away beneath him, he collapsed to the floor, along with the remaining members of the council.

She darted forward and clambered over the broken remains of the council bench, looking for her prey.

The room was a mess. She waded through the battered wreckage, finding herself in the walking space behind the council's elaborate bench. She could see where they entered the hall and then climbed a short series of stairs to reach the bench.

As Kasey took in her surroundings, a flicker of motion caught her eye. She ducked instinctively as the shimmering silver blade cut through the air where her head had been only moments ago.

The Shinigami snarled. The short sword lashed out again and again, but Kasey ducked and wove. The blade was far from the perfect weapon for the confined space. The wood work inhibited some of his motion, but the master of the Shinigami was relentless. Slash by slash, he harried Kasey through the space. Step-by-step, she danced back out of reach.

As the Shinigami closed, Kasey felt something at her back. It was the wall.

She'd run out of space.

The Shinigami smiled as he thrust home the blade. The blade drove through the air toward Kasey's stomach.

Kasey sidestepped the blade at the last moment. Grabbing the Shinigami's wrist with both her hands, she took control of the weapon. The Shinigami might have been a wizard for longer than she'd been alive, but Kasey had spent more time in the ring than most people twice her age, and she was fighting for her life.

She twisted his wrist and slammed his hand into the wall. The Shinigami's shield did nothing against the mundane assault. She slammed his hand into the wall again, and bones cracked. The blade fell to the floor, its point burying into the wooden boards.

The Shinigami wrenched back his broken hand. She swung at him, and her blow thundered into his chest. She drew back her right fist, planning to lay him out cold.

The Shinigami raised his good hand and chanted, "*Bakufuu!*"

She was too close to dodge the attack. The blast of energy knocked her off her feet. She found herself hurtling back through the broken wood work into the courtroom. She hit the ground hard, the wind driven from her lungs. Ringing filled her head.

She tried to breathe but her lungs burned. She felt like she'd been kicked by a horse and it ached all over.

Digging deep, she willed herself on. With Akihiro in her sights, nothing was going to keep her down. Fighting the pain, she raised herself onto her hands and knees. Then, one leg at a time, she stood up. Her mother ran toward her, as Sanders stormed into the breach. Kasey struggled to keep on her feet.

Her mother reached her. "Where does it hurt, Kasey?"

Kasey winced. "Everywhere."

Her mother placed a hand on Kasey's shoulder and whispered an incantation. As the arcane energy rolled over Kasey a surging warmth filled her being. At its embrace, her taut and aching muscles loosened as the weariness of her week washed from her.

"How's that?" her mother asked.

"Fantastic." Kasey replied, rolling her shoulders. "I feel better than I have in days."

"Good. That'll help for now. Remember, magic may bend the rules but never break them. Your body is a bow that will eventually snap. You need rest."

"No. I need to catch the Shinigami before he escapes. This ends today." Kasey turned as Sanders emerged from the wood work.

"He's gone," Sanders said. "He slipped out through the council's chambers. We need to lock down the building."

He grabbed the nearest ADI agent by the front of his shirt. The agent had been watching the fight unfold, too dumbfounded to react. He looked at Sanders and blinked, his thoughts clear on his face: on the one hand, he had orders to apprehend Director Sanders, but on the other, he had seen Arthur Ainsley transform into some sort of Japanese killing machine.

Sanders shook him. "Wake up! That man is responsible for the murder of Theo Getz and he's just killed half the council before your very eyes. I need you to seal the building."

"But we have orders to..."

"I don't care what your orders are. Give me your earpiece, now."

The man shook but didn't make any move.

Sanders dropped him. Reaching down, he ripped the man's earpiece free. The man reached for his weapon.

"I wouldn't do that, agent. I'm not the enemy here, but if you touch that gun, it'll be the last thing you do. You either help us or get the hell out of our way, but there is no middle ground. Not today."

The agent relaxed and lowered his hands. Sanders reached down and took the gun for good measure. After tucking it into his pants, he fixed the earpiece behind his ear.

"Agents of the ADI, this is your director, Noah Sanders. Seal the building at once. I know you have orders to detain me at any cost, but as you will soon learn there is a hostile power loose in the Council Chambers. The man we believe to be Arthur Ainsley has been a wolf in our midst. The truth is, our friend Arthur died over a year ago and this impostor has been leading us astray ever since. If you come into contact with Arthur Ainsley, you are to detain him at all costs. If you see an oriental man in a silk robe, approach with caution. Consider him armed and extremely dangerous. The intruder is the Master of the Shinigami. He has already killed several council members. We need medical teams from the Administorum to the Council Chambers immediately. No non-ADI agents are to enter into the Councils' private sanctum."

Sanders paced as he barked his instructions. "We believe the hostile is hiding inside the sanctum. Evacuate all non-essential personnel, ensure that you use a revelation spell on them before allowing them to leave the building. The intruder cannot be allowed to leave. I repeat, he is armed and extremely dangerous. He poses an imminent threat not only to us but the entire city. He must be contained at any cost. If you have any doubt of the truth of what I speak, simply watch the closed circuit footage of the court's proceedings. You will see the impostor clearly revealed and you will see him murder many of the Arcane Council in cold blood. You know me. I have and will always act in the best interest of this body. All willing hands are welcome but know that if you raise your hand against me today, in the best interest of our people, I will have to go straight through you. Stand with us or stay out of my way."

Sanders looked at Kasey and her mother, exasperation creasing his forehead. "Surveillance department, this is Sanders. Please isolate the footage from the court proceedings and play it on every display throughout the building. Play it on a loop. We need everyone to be aware of the danger posed by this man. Agents, seal off the twenty-fifth floor. Converge on the Sanctum and bring the full weight of our agency down on his head."

Kasey approached one of the other nearby ADI agents and held out her hand. "Give me your earpiece, now."

The agent looked from her to Sanders and then back to her.

"What are you waiting for?" she asked. "I'm your best chance of catching this man before he kills anyone else. I need to hear what you're hearing."

The agent reached up and took his earpiece out before handing it to Kasey. She jammed it into her ear.

The channel was quiet.

Agent Sanders' entreaty seemed to have fallen on deaf ears. Kasey waited in silence as the seconds ground by. With each passing moment, her anxiety grew. Surely now after everything they had been through, they wouldn't have to continue to contend with the ADI. She'd been here once before, less than ten days ago. The thought of having to fight her way out of the building once more was more than she could bear. Tears threatened to roll down her cheeks.

There was a cackle of static as the channel came to life. "Director Sanders, this is the surveillance office. We've seen the footage. It's hard to watch, sir."

"Indeed," Sanders replied. "I saw it with my own eyes and am still struggling with it, but I need you to..."

"Don't worry, director," the voice interrupted. "It's already playing on all screens. If anyone hasn't seen it yet, they soon will."

Kasey's heart leapt at the announcement. Finally, something was going their way.

"Thank you, agent," Sanders replied

"No, sir. Thank you. It's good to have you back."

Sanders nodded as he took in the battered courtroom. "It's good to be back, but I fear the worst is still ahead of us."

# CHAPTER 20

Kasey burst through the door into the Council Sanctum. The ADI were attempting to seal the Council Complex. Their best chance to catch Akihiro was before he reached the surface. Kasey's own experience escaping the Arcane Council told her that once he was out of the Council Chambers, there would be very little the Arcane Council could do to block every entrance and exit to the metropolis.

Moreover, once he was clear of the Council Chambers, masquerading as Arthur Ainsley, most of the magical community wouldn't think twice about letting him pass. Indeed, if they were to stand a chance at stopping him, they would have to catch him before he reached the surface.

Kasey found herself in a richly furnished corridor. Two ADI agents lay unmoving on the floor. She checked for a pulse. There was none whatsoever. Whatever spell the Master had used, it had done its work effectively. The two had never stood a chance.

Kasey advanced down the corridor with Sanders and her mother only a single stride behind. She had to go for a happy medium between headlong pursuit and blindly meandering into a trap set by Akihiro. He'd proved himself a more than capable adversary and if they continued without due care, they might find themselves like the two agents they had just passed.

Akihiro had shown he had no regard for human life. If anything, he had shown a relish for the taking of it. Not surprising, considering what he had planned for the city. Some part of her had hoped the crowded courtroom might contain his response. Unfortunately, she had been mistaken. It was a miracle more people hadn't been slain in the confrontation.

Reaching for the office doors, Kasey began opening each of them. She started on the left with Noah taking those on the right.

The offices were the sitting chambers for members of the Council. In this private sanctum, they could deliberate and carry on the affairs of the council without interference from the vast bureaucracy above them. Freed from interruption, they governed the affairs of the World of Magic in the United States.

*Until today.*

Each door she opened revealed a large private office space. The furnishings differed by room, but most were dominated by a large mahogany desk and shelves lined with books and manuscripts running along the walls.

Each office was empty. She reached the last door. It was labeled Arthur Ainsley, Arcane Chancellor.

She stood poised, ready to throw open the door. Noah took up position behind her, gun in hand. She could feel the tendrils of arcane energy gather as her mother raised both hands, ready to unleash hell.

Kasey threw open the door, and Sanders stormed into the room. Kasey was hot on his heels. An ornamental Ming vase held pride of place in the corner of the chamber. Several portraits in gold frames hung behind the desk. They depicted people Kasey didn't recognize, but she presumed they were past Chancellors who had held the office. The pictures spanned back generations.

"Empty," Sanders declared. "I think he's already made a break for the surface."

"Then we best be after him," Kasey said, sweeping her hair behind her ear. "We can't rely on the ADI to contain him. We escaped from here, it's safe to assume he can, too."

"What's the most direct route to the surface?" her mother asked. "The ADI will be trying to evacuate the rest of the building. Anyone who hasn't heard what transpired down here is just going to let him pass. We need to get to him, now."

"There is a bank of elevators from these Chambers to the Underpass. It allows the counselors to come and go as they will, without the need to wait for anyone else," Sanders said.

"Lead the way." Kasey pointed to the door.

Sanders strode out of the office and down the hall, never at any point lowering his weapon. As they reached the bank of elevators, one was climbing steadily toward the surface. The other waited idly.

Kasey mashed the elevator's button furiously. The doors parted and she charged into the elevator, Sanders and her mother right behind her.

"Which floor?" Kasey asked.

"The Underpass," Sanders replied. "It's the surest way out of here. Also has the largest crowd for him to get lost in. Remember, he could be anyone by now, not just Ainsley."

Kasey punched the button for the Underpass, and the elevator rocketed toward the surface.

The security monitor in the elevator was playing a constant reel of the scene that had unfolded in the courtroom. Kasey watched in horror once more as the Shinigami killed the council member at his side. It seemed the surveillance team was spreading the message far and wide.

The Shinigami would have his work cut out for him. His Arthur Ainsley alibi wouldn't hold up to scrutiny for much longer now. Kasey let out a deep breath as she tried to calm her pounding heart. It threatened to leap out of her chest.

She was so close. Her visions, the attack on the city, the killings—everything had led her to this point. The man behind it all had finally been revealed, and now he was running for his life. It felt good to be the hunter rather than the hunted for once. Now with the resources of the ADI severed, the Master of the Shinigami was alone and outnumbered.

*It all ends today.*

The doors opened and Kasey leapt out of the elevator into the Underpass. The elevators opened directly onto the concourse. As they stepped out into the expansive chamber, people fled in disarray. Screams echoed down the corridor.

"I guess we know which way he went," Kasey said to Sanders.

"Indeed. He's not running. He's hurting our people."

"It's to be expected," her mother replied. "You weren't alive for the fifties. It was a dangerous time to be in New York. The Council had waned under weak leadership and mobs of wizards roamed the streets. Those wizards ruled through fear and oppression.

We have robbed Akihiro of his army, Kasey. Now he seeks to maintain his power through intimidation and fear."

"Not if I have anything to say about it," Kasey said. "It's time we put him in the ground for good."

She took off down the Underpass, chasing the chaos unfolding ahead. The footsteps of Sanders and her mother pounded behind her.

As they ran, a voice in her ear called a warning. "Director Sanders, we're under attack."

"Under attack?" Sanders answered. "In the Underpass? Yes, we are aware of it. We're moving to intercept the suspect as we speak."

There was a pause. "No, sir. I mean, yes, sir. We are aware the chief suspect is in the Underpass wreaking havoc. I'm speaking about the force that has broken in from outside. They have breached our blockade at City Hall."

"City Hall? What the...? Tell me more, now!"

"As you instructed, director, we've stationed men at every exit. Our agents at City Hall just radioed in that they have run into hostile fire. An unknown party of wizards attacked them from the streets. They were heavily armed and employing magic with abandon. Sir, they are on the streets, in full view of the public."

"We can't worry about that now," Sanders replied. "We'll do whatever damage control we can later. For now, we need to apprehend Akihiro. Any idea how many of them there are?"

The surveillance office replied, "Dozens, sir. I tried to raise our agents again, but neither of them are responding. Is it safe to assume these intruders are acting in concert with our suspect?"

Sanders looked up the Underpass. They were heading for Town Hall.

"Without a doubt. They have come to extract him. We can't be far behind, but we are going to need backup. There are three of us and one of him, but we can't deal with dozens of his allies. Have all agents converge on the Underpass, we need to reach him before they do. If they breached at City Hall, that will be their extraction point. We need to trap him here. If he makes it to the streets, there's no telling what they'll do."

"Roger that. We'll rally our forces," the voice replied.

The call for reinforcements went out over the earpiece. At least this time the agents were on their side.

Sanders stopped and pulled out his phone. He began hastily dialing a number.

Kasey came to a halt next to him. "Sanders, what are you doing?"

"Calling for reinforcements," he replied cryptically.

The line opened, but she didn't recognize the voice at the other end.

"It's me," Sanders began. "The target is in the tunnels beneath City Hall. He's likely shed his alias and may no longer be pretending to be the Arcane Chancellor. You'll know him when you see him. Oriental man in his mid to late fifties. He'll be at the heart of the carnage. Take him down."

"Understood. Moving to intercept," the voice replied.

Sanders hung up the phone and slid it back into his pocket. "Hades' men. I figure every man will count and they're as ruthless as anyone I've ever met."

Kasey nodded. It made sense. After all, they had spent a million in cash to secure Hades' assistance. It would be nice to see some sort of payoff from her time in the cage.

The three of them stormed down the Underpass. As they moved down the tunnels, they found two agents huddling behind a marble statue of a witch Kasey didn't recognize.

"Director," the first agent shouted, leaping to his feet.

The second joined him

Sanders hurried to them. "Tell me what's going on."

"It's the chancellor," the first agent said, panting. "He's gone ballistic. He's butchering anyone that gets in his path."

"That's not the chancellor. He's a rogue agent who had infiltrated the council. We need to take him down immediately."

The agents fell into step behind them. From the creases of worry on their faces, Kasey could see they were less than enthusiastic about attacking the man they had previously believed to be the Chancellor of the Arcane Council.

A piercing scream echoed down the Underpass. They quickened their pace. Kasey could feel the steady pounding of her heart as she drew each breath. Up ahead, the Master of the Shinigami appeared. He was disguised as Arthur Ainsley once more. One hand was raised, and two ADI agents hovered in the air before him. The agents danced like marionettes on a string, their bodies twitching as they were tortured by unseen hands.

Arthur advanced down the corridor, waving his arms like the deranged conductor of a deadly symphony.

Innocent bystanders cowered before the impostor.

Kasey knew that kind of fear. She'd felt it herself, when she was being hunted. It was the same terror that had rooted her to the spot as she had stared into the gaping maw of the werewolf, Danilo.

With one sweep of his hand, the Chancellor cast the bystanders aside like rag dolls. The bystanders bounced along the Underpass, before sliding into a heap against the wall.

Kasey longed to help them, but the Master of the Shinigami had to be stopped first. She quickened her pace. The Master must've heard their approach as he turned and looked over his shoulder.

"Oh, the insufferable Kasey Chase and Mr. Sanders. I'm surprised you are willing to bring yourself within my reach once more. You two truly are the worst excuses for heroes I've ever seen. Don't you realize you stand before the tsunami? It will crush you and everything else before it. You can't stop us now, it's too late."

Kasey summoned her power, but before the words of her spell could even leave her lips, a lance of blue energy emanated from somewhere to her right. The spell scored a glancing hit to the Master's shoulder. He howled in rage, as the attack shattered his concentration and burned into his shoulder.

Kasey followed the source of the spell and saw John Ainsley advancing on the Master.

Kasey had no idea where John had emerged from, but given his father's position, she had no doubt he knew the complex rabbit warren of tunnels beneath Manhattan as well as anyone alive. Most people would have used them to flee. John had used them to hunt down his father's killer.

John chanted again and a blast of energy rolled toward the Master. The Master's left arm may have hung uselessly from his ruined shoulder, but his right hand rose to meet it.

The two agents that had been dancing before him crumpled to the floor as the Chancellor turned his whole focus on John. Akihiro chanted, and John dodged reflexively.

In spite of the Master's chanting there was no arcane missile to evade. Instead, John was torn from his feet by the same incantation the Master of the Shinigami had used to control the agents.

Kasey gasped as John was swept from his feet. Waving his hand like the conductor of some macabre symphony, the Master of the Shinigami dragged John through the air until he stood suspended between Akihiro and Kasey.

"Miss Chase, go ahead and unleash that spell. You will likely hit your beloved."

Kasey felt the arcane energy coursing through her. Every fiber of her being wanted to let loose and obliterate the Master of the Shinigami, but she knew that no matter how she aimed her spell, he would ensure John was first to be hit.

She would be killing John herself. The thought tore at her heartstrings. She didn't know how to process her feelings for him anymore. Once, he'd been her tormentor, but more recently he'd been her ally, her confidant, and friend. She'd even come to enjoy the little time they had manage to spend together. They were feelings that she had never expected.

She had no idea how to diffuse the situation without putting him in harm's way.

"What do we do?" Kasey asked Sanders, unable to look away from John. "We can't let him go, but we can't attack him either. Whatever we do, John is bound to get caught in the crossfire."

"I'm not playing with you, Miss Chase," the Master of the Shinigami said. "One more step, one more spell, one more misguided breath in my direction and I'll end his existence before your very eyes."

Kasey stood rooted to the spot. It was John, or the city. She could see the outcome with perfect clarity. If they let Akihiro leave, he would destroy New York City. If they didn't, he would kill John. He'd killed dozens already; she had no doubt John would be next if they did not comply.

Akihiro had put her in this position before, though she hadn't known him at the time. It had been Langstrode or Bishop. She could only save one. He knew all too well how she would react. She'd chosen Bishop over Langstrode and allowed the Shinigami to further his plans. In her heart she knew there was a price to be paid to save the city, but she could not bear to watch another pay it.

"Take me," Kasey said, voice even.

"No, Kasey!" her mother cried out.

Kasey held up a hand for silence. "Take me in his place. I'm the one you wanted anyway, right? You sent Danilo after me. It was me that killed your little cabals of murderers. I'm the one you want, not him. What is he to you? Let him go and take me as your collateral."

"I'm not here to bargain, Miss Chase."

"But you should," Kasey countered. "I might not be willing to risk his life, but Sanders and his agents aren't going to think twice. Not after today."

Akihiro nodded. "It is certainly a tempting proposition. After all, without you, none of us would even be standing here today. I accept. Come, slowly. I'm warning you, one step out of place, one breath of a spell upon your lips, and I will end him, and you will have a front row seat."

Kasey raised her hands, "It's not a ploy, Akihiro. I'm simply sick of seeing others pay the price."

She advanced toward the Chancellor.

Her mother tried to reach for her. "No, Kasey. You can't do this."

Kasey shook her off.

"Kasey, don't do it," Sanders said, but didn't dare to move.

Kasey paused, looking over her shoulder at her mother and Sanders. "I can, and I will. You know everything I know about his plot now. If he escapes, you know where to go." Her gaze fixed on her mother. "Momma, I love you. You're the best mother a girl could ever ask for. I'm sorry I couldn't do more."

Kasey couldn't ever recall seeing her mother flustered. Now, she watched as her mother's stern expression broke like a dam shattering. Tears welled up in her eyes.

It was more than Kasey could take. She turned and continued to walk toward the Master of the Shinigami.

She felt the weight of the world pressing down on her shoulders as she neared John.

John was shaking in the air. Whatever spell Akihiro was using to immobilize him, John was fighting with every fiber of his being.

As soon as Kasey got within a few steps of him, the Shinigami flipped his hand. John sailed up into the roof.

"No!" Kasey screamed as he struck the ceiling and then hurtled downward into the tiles.

Before Kasey could reach for him, she felt an icy grip surround her. Akihiro had her and she knew it. Kasey looked at the crumpled form of John Ainsley as she was swept into the air.

The chill seemed to completely enshroud her. It felt as if she were diving deep underwater. The pressure threatened to crush in on her from every direction. The Shinigami was literally squeezing the life out of her.

Kasey hovered through the air until she rested helplessly before him.

Akihiro's mouth widened into a smile. "Well, well, well, Miss Chase. What are we to do with you now?"

# Chapter 21

Kasey hovered helplessly in the air, dangling before the Master of the Shinigami. All over her body, she could feel the weight of her arcane containment crushing against her. It was slowly, inexorably squeezing the life out of her. At her feet, John Ainsley lay in a heap.

Akihiro, Master of The Shinigami, grinned maniacally as he used the floating Kasey as a human shield.

"Now, just give me a moment to take care of this shoulder and we shall be out of here, Miss Chase," the Shinigami said. He glanced back at her mother and Sanders. "Not a move out of either of you two, or I swear you will see her die in a manner so excruciatingly painful, you will never be able to erase it from your mind. Imagine her bursting like an overfilled balloon. I promise you, it's a sight you will never forget."

The Shinigami chanted as he laid his good hand over his ruined shoulder. The suit his illusion was wearing had been blasted apart, and blood stained his shirt.

As Akihiro chanted, sickly emerald energy emanated from his palm and washed over his shoulder. Kasey's eyes widened. She had expected the same healing glow her mother used on her earlier. The master must've seen her surprised reaction because he looked up and offered a pitying smile.

"You see, Kasey, the problem with using magic to heal is that you are trying to use an arcane force to heal a failing mortal frame. Not a bad option if you have no other choice. But for those versed in necromancy, the art of life and death, it is a poor second choice. Far better to restore life with life."

Kasey's eyes descended to the glowing talisman around his neck.

"Yes, precisely. This device allows me to capture the energy that escapes from a person's body at the moment they expire. Stored and preserved, that life force allows me to extend my own life far beyond that of a normal mortal. You are all positively infantile to me. I have seen centuries come and go. You are so attracted to this ideal of freedom, you have no comprehension of how the world works. America is just another pretender momentarily occupying the center of the world stage. I watched as your country rose and I'll be the instrument of its fall. There is no stopping us now."

Kasey watched as the ruined flesh knit itself together. When he was done, the skin of his shoulder looked unblemished, it was as if he'd never been wounded at all.

Footsteps thudded behind her, dozens upon dozens. All around her, the ADI was converging on their location. More seemed to be approaching from behind the Master of the Shinigami.

Her heart leapt.

The Master of the Shinigami was about to be completely surrounded and cut off from his escape. She may have had little chance of survival, but it was comforting to know that he would die too.

As the agents approached, Kasey studied them. Something was wrong; they were far too at ease. They advanced, completely unconcerned by the presence of Arthur Ainsley surrounded by the bodies of dozens of civilians and their fellow agents. Their faces were an unreadable facade.

Each agent carried an MP5 submachine gun. It wasn't standard issue for the ADI, though it was a weapon that she had been on the receiving end of before. The same weapon carried by the Shinigami and their acolytes during the assault on the Ninth Precinct.

Kasey realized what was happening.

Those standing behind the Master were no agents of the ADI. They were not salvation. They were Akihiro's reinforcements and they were disguised as ADI agents. The unknown force that had stormed City Hall was here.

Kasey looked to their arms. The mark of the Shinigami was inked just above the right wrist. She wanted to scream a warning, but she could not move. She prayed that Sanders would see it in time.

"It's time for us to leave, Kasey," the Master of the Shinigami declared. "Say goodbye to your friends. If you're lucky, they might live through the day, but then again, you never know. It always pays to be prepared."

Kasey hovered in the air, completely unable to speak.

"What's the matter, Kasey? Cat got your tongue?" Akihiro laughed. The maniacal tone resonated eerily down through the corridor.

As he drank in his victory, Kasey noticed movement at her feet. It was John.

His eyes fluttered open. He squinted up at the Shinigami. Slowly, John reached behind his back. The hilt of a pistol peeked out from his pants.

It seemed he was favoring the gun over magic as to avoid detection. Doubtless the Master of the Shinigami would have felt the buildup of energy as John rallied his might for a sudden onslaught. The pistol at this range would prove just as deadly and provide no warning.

Just as the pistol cleared John's pants, the Master swung around to face him. The master chanted, and a blade appeared in his hands. Unlike the short sword he'd been using earlier, this one was long and slender, almost a needle but for its length. With uncanny speed, the Master of the Shinigami brought the blade down.

Kasey had seen the weapon before, in her vision of the cathedral. It was the same blade she had seen used on Arthur Ainsley.

With her eyes fixed in terror, Kasey watched in slow motion as John brought up the pistol. The blade descended as John leveled the pistol at the Master's face.

The slender blade drove straight through John's chest.

As the blade took him in the heart, Kasey's own broke.

The gunshot never came. The Master of the Shinigami grinned down at John. "Oh, I know you so very badly want to pull that trigger, but you see, the Night Blade paralyzes its victim. It allows them to enjoy one brief moment of utter helplessness before they expire. There's a kind of beautiful symmetry when you think about it. In this moment, you have more in common with your father than ever before. This is the same blade that killed him and now it will be your death too."

John lips pursed in pain.

"Kasey!" he gasped.

An emerald hue traveled from John's chest, along the blade, and into the Master of the Shinigami. The Shinigami was draining John's life force.

"Waste not, want not," Akihiro said.

Kasey watched in agony as John's head sank lifelessly against the tiles of the Underpass. She wanted to cry out but could not, her every move restrained by the suffocating spell she was encased in. Her eyes burned as the tears welled up. John had died without ever hearing how she felt.

A gunshot split the silence in the Underpass.

The unseen hands that had held her fast were gone, and Kasey fell to the floor.

She hit the tiles in a crumpled heap, pain shooting through her leg. She pushed herself upright and looked over her shoulder. Sanders had his gun raised, a faint whiff of smoke rising from its barrel. She glanced over at the Master. Blood pooled on his shirt. As the Master of the Shinigami had killed John, he must have stepped out from behind the cover that Kasey had afforded him.

Sanders had taken the only shot he had.

With one hand, he tried to stem the bleeding in his chest. He began chanting.

Sanders opened fire once more, round after round straight at the Master. This time, Sanders had a clean shot. He was shooting to kill.

An emerald shield encased the Master and Sanders' bullets flattened uselessly against the protective shell.

The gun clicked. He was empty.

The fake agents raised their weapons in unison.

Kasey was only feet away. It was too late for her. At this distance, she would never manage a shield in time. She simply collapsed on top of John and cried.

The restrained tears burst from her like a river as she wept.
Closing her eyes, she buried her face in John's chest and waited for the end. The fusillade was deafening as the Shinigami acolytes raised their weapons and unleashed hell.

# CHAPTER 22

Kasey wept openly. Tears rolled down her cheeks as her world ended around her. The deafening staccato fire of automatic weapons filled the Underpass and Kasey could feel the ebb and flow of magical current washing all around her.

The agents returned fire against the Shinigami acolytes. Their handguns might have been outmatched by the MP5s but the agents responded with enough arcane firepower to level a small city.

Amid it all, Kasey simply buried her head against John's shoulder. She wanted to try and heal him, but she knew it was too late. Checking his pulse, her fears were confirmed. He was gone. Even magic wouldn't bring back the dead.

At any moment, she expected she would join him. Surely the deadly hail of bullets would find her.

Kasey closed her eyes again and waited for the end to come.

All around her, the battle raged and yet she remained unscathed.

Looking up, Kasey forced her eyes open. Shimmering over her head was a protective scarlet shield. In the furious melee she could not see its origin, but she knew it all the same.

It was her mother.

There was only one person in the Underpass who would put her life above their own. Somewhere amid the chaos, her mother had woven a powerful protective barrier around Kasey.

Kasey looked behind her at an ever-increasing flow of agents joining the battle. Glancing ahead, she could make out the contingent of Shinigami acolytes fortifying the Underpass. They were taking cover behind statues and benches before returning fire.

Kasey scanned the area for the Master but he was nowhere to be seen. His flight had been swift and now his acolytes were selling their lives to buy him time to escape.

Kasey was tired. Physically and emotionally, she was utterly spent. She had come so far and in spite of all of her efforts to protect him, John had paid the ultimate price. Her soul ached, but she knew that she couldn't languish in self-pity and loathing forever. Not while the Master of the Shinigami lived to fight another day.

Akihiro had to die.

Kasey quarantined the feelings that threatened to consume her. There would be a time to mourn, but it would have to wait.

She laid a hand on John's chest.

*He will pay for this. They will all pay for this.*

She rose to one knee and then struggled to her feet. The Shinigami turned on her, their weapons pointed at her at point blank range. Placing her faith in her protector, she unleashed her rage in torrents of arcane destruction. With no mercy, she moved through the Shinigami like a hurricane.

Bullets ricocheted harmlessly off her protective shield, producing the faintest wisps of scarlet light before they clattered harmlessly to the ground.

"*Chwythu Asid!*" Kasey bellowed in her Celtic tongue.

A searing blast of violet light streamed from her outstretched hands. In a heartbeat, the wave of energy had scythed through three acolytes. They collapsed in a heap to rise no more.

Other Shinigami brought their weapons to bear on her, but her shield held. She looked into the eyes of her nearest enemy. The surprise was written across his face, until another emotion replaced it. His eyes went wide, his jaw dropped, and his expression told Kasey he knew what was coming next.

Weaving her arms, she lashed out once more. This time the violet scythe cleaved the man in half.

His comrades watched him fall and looked to the avatar of destruction in their midst. Kasey was the eye of the storm all around her.

Buoyed by Kasey's presence, the ADI pressed forward.

Sanders shouted over the din. "Advance. We need Akihiro. Beat them back, drive them back at once."

The ADI surged forward.

A fireball sailed past her and exploded into a pair of acolytes who were reloading. Kasey pressed onward. Lightning cackled from her outstretched palms, striking Shinigami on either side of her. The Shinigami crumpled to the earth, and Kasey continued her advance.

Up ahead, a handful of acolytes had taken shelter behind a water fountain. From the cover of the fountain stonework, they laid down a withering hail of fire. The ADI traded shots with the suit-clad acolytes unsuccessfully.

Kasey opted for a more direct approach.

Racing at the emplacement, Kasey ignored the hail of fire reflecting off her shield and vaulted up onto the ledge of the fountain.

For a split second, Kasey allowed herself to enjoy the intricately carved center piece of the fountain. A trio of mermaids lounged on a stone outcropping that had been carved into the shape of a reef. Water streamed out of the stonework, before landing in the fountain to be recycled. It was an impressive sight.

Their fate would be a crying shame.

Kasey had learned a trick or two from her encounter with the gargoyles. "*Hud Ysgarlad.*"

A lance of scarlet arcane energy leapt from her palms and hit the centerpiece. For a moment, the lance just seemed to disappear into the stonework, without effect. Then, the stonework began to glow. Cracks appeared in the surface of the stone, racing out from the point of impact. There was a deafening blast as the superheated stone exploded like a frag grenade.

Shrapnel rained down on the Shinigami acolytes. With the centerpiece obliterated, Kasey's lance struck the fountain edge the acolytes cowered behind. The masonry shattered outward. The weight of the water bowled over the Shinigami who hadn't already been laid low by the withering hail of stone shrapnel.

With the acolytes dispersed, the ADI advanced.

Kasey reveled in her success, but motion to her right drew her eye. She turned as an emerald orb hurtled toward her face.

The shield took the worst of the brunt, but the power of the blast still threw Kasey clear off her perch. She struck the tiles hard, the impact winding her. She struggled for breath but her relief at surviving the blast faded as her shield shimmered once and then failed, collapsing in on itself and her.

Kasey was completely exposed.

The Shinigami acolyte smirked as he raised his hands to deliver the killing blow, but a withering hail of gunfire drove him into cover.

Kasey shook herself off and got to her feet. She owed her life to the ADI agents surging before her. If not for their cover fire, she would surely be dead.

Mindful of the fact that Akihiro was slipping away with every moment, Kasey raised both hands and bellowed, *"Pêl Tân."*

Fire leapt from her outstretched hands. The blaze closed the distance between her and the Shinigami acolyte. Before the flames could strike their target, an emerald latticework of energy spread before them. The latticework raced outward with the Shinigami acolyte at its center. The latticework spread until it stretched from him to fill the door frame. The Shinigami and his shield now completely obscured the path forward.

Kasey's enchantment washed over the latticework but faded, leaving the shield intact.

"He is blocking the Master's escape," Sanders shouted above the fray. "We need to break through, and we need to do it now. Agents, give it everything you've got."

Sanders and his army of agents unleashed their arcane might on the barrier.

One agent leveled a bolt of lightning at the barrier. Others sent lances of arcane energy of varying shades. Kasey understood their intent at once. Utilizing a shield enchantment drained the energy of the user. The more energy that was deflected, the greater the strain on the magic user. No wizard could hold out indefinitely. Even the most powerful ward would eventually fail as its caster succumbed to fatigue.

Outnumbered dozens to one, the acolyte's sacrifice was inevitable. He was fighting a losing battle. It was his life in exchange for his master. Kasey watched as the acolyte began to sweat. Agent after agent blasted away at the barrier, two or three enchantments at a time. Worry wrinkles formed on the acolyte's brow as the strain of maintaining the spell increased.

Kasey hurled another fireball at the barrier.

The latticework slowly dimmed. The acolyte was shaking visibly and sweat ran down his brow. His smile was gone now. He knew his fate was set in stone.

Seeing the fatigue, Kasey summoned her energy once more and bellowed, *"Anymwybodol."*

She hurled the sleep enchantment at the Shinigami. Eventually, the shield would break but Kasey hoped a less direct assault might slip through the wavering ward. The unseen energy rolled toward the Shinigami like an ocean tide. Slowly, inexorably, it moved onward. Then, it struck him.

The Shinigami faltered. His hands dropped to his side. His eyes closed as he teetered on his feet. His knees gave out and he dropped. Before he could hit the ground, the next agent's spell struck him. The lightning bolt took him in the torso and passed through him, grounding itself at his feet. There was enough power to stop his heart instantly. The Shinigami was dead before he hit the ground.

The shield disappeared completely.

Kasey ran forward. Leaving the agents to deal with the remnants of the Shinigami forces, she raced through the door the acolyte had died guarding. Footsteps pounded behind her, and she turned. Sanders was hot on his heels.

"Don't worry, it's just me. Let's take him," Sanders said.

Kasey nodded and lengthened her stride. Akihiro was close; she could feel it. The greatest threat the city had ever known, he'd been exposed and now he lay within her grasp. It was time to end him and his plot once and for all.

She sprinted along the corridor. It was unfurnished. Painted bricks lined the walls, an interesting contrast to the old linoleum surface of the floors.

Straight ahead hung a sign: City Hall.

Sanders guess had been right. The Master of the Shinigami was taking the most direct exit and making for the street.

Kasey threw open a steel door. It resembled a fire exit. The door opened onto a landing with a set of concrete stairs leading upward.

She began racing up them two at a time. She panted as she climbed flight after flight of concrete stairs. Reaching the third floor above the Underpass, she came to an unlabeled door. Opening it, she found herself in an office. The room was furnished but a thin layer of dust coating the desk told her it hadn't been used in years.

Sanders was right behind her. The door clicked shut, and Kasey realized it had locked.

Leaving the office, Kasey sprinted down the hall. City Hall was deserted. Together, they made quick progress towards the exit. Reaching the lobby, Kasey stopped dead. The historic and pristine entrance to City Hall had been destroyed. The iconic doors had been blasted off their hinges and lay shattered in the entryway.

The Shinigami acolytes had made a direct assault. The lobby had been utterly destroyed. Bodies lay everywhere. One head had been severed from its body. Another had been cleft in twain. Two of the bodies looked like they had been cooked alive, while another appeared to have been crushed until his entire body had been compressed until it was the same shape and size as a basketball.

"What happened here?" Kasey asked, studying the bodies. "These don't look like the ADI."

They were dressed in black from head to toe and wearing bullet-proof vests. The group carried an assortment of automatic weapons.

"Are they Shinigami?" she asked, bending down to check their forearms for tattoos. There was nothing. "No, whoever these men were, they were not with the Shinigami."

Sanders crouched over a lifeless body that stared vacantly at the ceiling.

"These are Hades' men. It seems they set their ambush here, but the Master was ready for them."

Kasey shook her head at the utter brutality of the assault. "I thought you said there were a dozen. Where are the rest?"

"I'm not sure," Sanders replied, scratching his head. "They should be here."

Shouting flooded in from the street. There was screaming, blaring car horns, and what sounded like a veritable stampede of people. Kasey raced through the destroyed lobby of City Hall, headed for the street.

She came out at the top of the stairs. Below, madness unfolded in downtown Manhattan. Two police cars were on fire. Nearby, one of the officers lay dead beside the open squad car's door.

She darted down the stairs. The ADI agents who had stood guard at City Hall's entrance lay dead on the ground. Both of them were riddled with bullets. The Shinigami had taken no prisoners in their breach.

All about her, pedestrians were milling about in panic. Kasey looked down Broadway Avenue. A crowd of pedestrians were fleeing toward her.

Beyond them, more than a dozen people hovered in the air.

Kasey tried to push northward up the street, but the throng of people rushing toward her threatened to crush her in the stampede.

A hand on her shoulder pulled her off the sidewalk and out of the path of the oncoming mob.

"It's no good, Kasey," Sanders said. "If you try to fight that, you'll be trampled to death. That, or you'll have to blast your way through innocent people."

Kasey studied the figures twisting and turning in the air and realized what they were. Several of them were the missing men from Hades' hit squad. At least three of them were wearing police uniforms. Others appeared to be innocent bystanders. All of them danced and turned in the air like puppets on a string.

Kasey felt for them. She'd been caught in the same enchantment only minutes ago and knew the utter helplessness of their situation.

Akihiro was terrorizing his way through downtown New York. The throng of traffic fleeing from him was too great. They would never catch up to him in time.

Kasey watched as the poor bystanders were caught in the brutal display.

With a collective scream, the floating figures plunged to the ground. They struck the road with a sickening thud.

The crowd cried out as it ran in every direction.

As the stampede thinned, Kasey and Sanders fought their way through the last vestiges of the mob. It was like swimming against the tide.

At last they found themselves at the intersection of Broadway and Chambers Street, where the bodies of those who had been tortured by Akihiro lay broken and discarded in the center of the street.

The Master of the Shinigami and his followers were nowhere to be seen.

Kasey and Sanders stood shaking their heads.

"Where is he?" Kasey asked.

"I have no idea," Sanders replied. "Doubtless he escaped in the chaos. There were thousands of people here. We need to face the truth. He's already gone."

Kasey slammed her hand on the hood of a parked taxi. They had been so close and yet he'd slipped through their fingers once more.

Sanders put his hand on her shoulder. "It's alright, Kasey. We'll get him yet. He's lost the council and he's been severely weakened. It's not all lost. We'll hunt him down."

"We're running out of time." Kasey dropped her face into her hands. "Any day now, they will destroy the city. Now that they know we are after them, it could happen any day. For all we know, it could be today. We need to stop him now!"

Sanders shook his head. "No, Kasey. Believe it or not, we have a bigger problem than the Shinigami."

Kasey looked up at him. "What do you mean?"

"I mean that." Sanders pointed to a half-dozen youths who stood filming the intersection on their smart phones.

Kasey's heart sank as the realization set in. The Shinigami's slaughter had happened in the middle of Manhattan in broad daylight. Not just the youths but doubtless hundreds if not thousands of others would have captured it on their cell phones. Any moment now, the footage would be all over the Internet.

The World of Magic was no longer a secret. Everyone with a screen and an internet connection would soon know about it. Their way of life, their society, everything they knew, had been exposed by the Master of the Shinigami in his sudden flight.

Today it was New York, but soon news would spread to the entire world. If the chaos unfolding around them was any indication, the world was not ready for wizardry.

"What do we do?" Kasey asked.

"There is nothing we can do. Even with the resources of the ADI, there is no way for us to stop it now. All we can do is try to contain with the fallout."

"New York City is a tinderbox on the best of days," Kasey replied. "Akihiro just struck a match and set it alight."

"So it seems," Sanders replied. "The Shinigami are more than willing to watch the world burn along with everyone in it. New York and the world as we know it, is about to draw its last breath."

Kasey shook her head. "No, Sanders. I won't give in. Not now. Not when we are so close. I'll take that last breath and hunt him down. Him, his cabal of murdering sociopaths, his plot to destroy the city. I'm going to end it all. Even if it's the last thing I ever do."

## The End

The secrets of the supernatural world have been exposed. Rogue wizards are marauding through the city and Kasey is out of time. She's put everything on the line for the city. Will it be enough?  Find out in *Until My Dying Day* (click here or scan the QR code below).

Or for the paperback version of Until My Dying Day click here (or scan the QR code below).

**Want more Kasey goodies?**

Sign up to my newsletter for some exclusive stories set in this world. You can join for free here (or scan the QR Code below) . You'll also be the first to hear about new releases, and other exciting news.

# YOU ARE THE DIFFERENCE

I hope you enjoyed the frantic pace of *One Last Breath.* The stage is set for a killer climax in *Until My Dying Day.* There is only days left until the Shinigami plot plunges New York City into ruin. Does Kasey and her fledgling band of heroes have what it takes to stop the attack? I guess we'll find out together in Until My Dying Day. In the meantime I have something to ask you.

As a self-published author, I don't have the huge marketing machine of a traditional publisher behind me. In fact, it's just me, my laptop and a half-empty packet of Tim Tams.

Fortunately for indie authors like me, we have incredible readers who make all the difference.

Every time you send a message or email, tell a friend about my series or share it on social media it helps me reach readers and continue to bring you more stories!

Also, your honest reviews of my books help other readers take a chance on me. It is the #1 thing you can do to help me (and Kasey) out.

If you have enjoyed this book, I would love it if you could spend a minute or two to leave a review for me. This link will take you there.

Thank you! I'll see you in Until My Dying Day. I hope you're ready for a frantic race to a very literal deadline.

Until next time!

S. C. Stokes

P.S. I know many readers are hesitant to reach out to an author, fearing that they might get ignored. I am a reader at heart and know how you feel. I respond to every Facebook message and every email I receive.

You can find me on:

Facebook
Bookbub
Email: samuel@samuelcstokes.com

You can also visit my website where you can join the VIP's and get a FREE EBOOK and other amazing goodies.

**Scroll on for a preview of Conjuring A Coroner 6: Until My Dying Day**

# PREVIEW - UNTIL MY DYING DAY

Kasey ran down the street, the chaos of New York City under siege drowning out each lengthy stride.

The mayor had issued the evacuation order, but it was already too late.

Emptying the bustling metropolis in a matter of hours was proving an impossible task. City traffic had come to a complete halt as the bottlenecked bridges cut Manhattan off from the mainland.

Drivers abandoned their cars and fled on foot. Tempers flared as an impatient mob began to form. Trapped in the city, fights began to break out, while others smashed windows in an attempt to vent their anger.

Pedestrians screamed as they sought safety amid the devastated city, but there was none to be found. The entire city shook beneath her feet as the buildings looming above her teetered and swayed. The movement was unsettlingly in the extreme.

Beneath her feet, the ground shook as great chasms yawned open along the street. Burst pipes leaked into the street as the seismic activity grew in intensity.

Nearby, a manhole cover exploded upward like a cork finally freed from its champagne bottle. The heavy iron cover flipped through the air until it smashed into the hood of a parked taxi.

From the broken cityscape, plumes of oily emerald smoke began to rise.

*It's happening. I am too late.*

Despite the freezing December air, beads of sweat ran down Kasey's brow. She had to keep running. So many lives depended on it. With his place on the Arcane Council taken from him and his identity unmasked, Akihiro had brought his plot to its devastating conclusion. Now, New York would pay the ultimate price.

The screech of tearing steel resounded from nearby. She slowed her pace and scanned her gaze in the direction of the noise.

The facade of the building beside her split open from the seismic upheaval. Windows shattered, raining glass down from above. Kasey shielded her face, but a large shard sliced into her left arm, drawing blood. She winced but there was little to be done now. As the building's structural integrity deteriorated, she picked up her pace. It would only be moments before the entire tower came crashing down.

Kasey tore her eyes from the building and focused on the street ahead.

A piercing wail split the evening air. It was far too shrill for an adult. When it came again, the scream cut straight to Kasey's heart.

She stopped, panting, and searched for source of the screams.

*It has to be a child.*

The scream carried above the din of the city. It was close.

Kasey leapt off the fractured sidewalk and into the street. The scream grew louder. Weaving through the traffic, Kasey spotted a sedan with its rear door open. A woman was leaning into the open door, and she seemed to be struggling with something in the back seat.

Kasey ran over to the sedan to find a young mother wrestling with her daughter's car seat. Tears ran down the mother's face as her shaking hands failed to shift the jammed buckle. As the daughter wailed, her mother only grew more frantic. Kasey pulled the mother aside and reached into the car. Grabbing the lock, she fought the mechanism. It wouldn't budge.

Out of time, Kasey whispered, *"Agored!"* The mechanism popped free and Kasey lifted the distraught toddler from the car.

Handing the child to her mother, she shouted, "Run! Get away from here now. The city is not safe. Head inland as quickly as you can."

The woman nodded, swiping tears from the child's cheeks.

"Thank you," she stammered.

She turned and bolted down the street, her child clasped against her chest.

Kasey watched her for a moment but tore her eyes away. There was nothing more she could do for her now.

Turning, Kasey ran in the opposite direction. The city was tearing itself apart, but a greater threat still approached. Determined to meet it head on, Kasey made for the bay.

At the traffic light, she turned right. Overhead, the sky was darkening, but it wasn't the setting sun. Boiling black clouds filled the air as they blended with the dense green smoke rising from the city. As they mixed, the clouds took on an emerald hue. Lightning played through the sky as thunder peeled overhead.

The storm was preparing to break, and it was unlike anything Kasey had ever seen. With her heart pounding in her ears at each loping stride, she ran for all she was worth. Her feet pounded against the sidewalk.

The earth shook again. Kasey staggered sideways, almost colliding with a trashcan. Wrapping herself around it, she steadied herself and waited for the tremors to subside.

She looked down the street. A yawning cleft had opened in the face of a towering residential building behind her. Although once a tower full of luxury apartments worth millions, none of that mattered now. The gaping wound in the building's face expanded in a rippling spiderweb of shattered steel and glass. The building swayed as it tore itself apart.

Kasey knew what came next. With the earth shaking underfoot, she darted through the crowd swarming away from its shuddering shadow. Terrified screams followed her up the street.

"The building, it's collapsing," a voice shouted over the chaos.

*They should run.*

Kasey pushed herself onward. A thunderous crack split the air as the broken building imploded on itself. Risking a glance over her shoulder, Kasey witnessed the dust cloud billowing out from its base.

She had to place more distance between herself and the building. The dust cloud would suffocate her in seconds. She continued to run.

The cloud billowed outward, racing down the street in every direction from the collapsing building. Kasey was already blocks away, but still it surged up the street behind her.

She ran until her side ached. With a deep breath, she looked over her shoulder. The dust's advance was slowing.

*That was close. Too close for comfort.*

Unfortunately, it wasn't the first building to come down and it wouldn't be the last. For all the destruction that had been visited upon the city, Kasey knew the worst was still to come.

She couldn't believe it had come to this. She'd fought so hard. With every fiber of her being she'd resisted them, but all about her the city told a different story. She had failed.

With more than a decade's warning in her visions, she'd still been powerless to stop the city she called home from being laid low and turned into a wasteland.

The storm broke overhead, and rain bore down on the city in heavy sheets. In moments, she was saturated. Her clothes clung to her as she ran onward.

She wept openly. The heavy tears rolled down her cheeks.

She had given it everything she knew how, and yet it had all come to nothing.

*Worse than nothing.*

She'd paid a terrible price for that failure. Her heart broke as she thought of John, bleeding out on the floor of the Underpass, her magic powerless to save him, as Akihiro loomed over him. The agony tore into her soul.

Now millions of others would know pain, and there was nothing she could do to stop it. In the distance, a deafening rumble signaled the collapse of another New York City superstructure.

Others would soon follow. They would be either laid low by the tremendous upheaval beneath them, or their collapse from the structural damage caused by the fall of the surrounding buildings. The city was interconnected, and each successive collapse would further weaken the city's urban superstructure.

The earth shook again. This time the seismic tremors were growing closer together. The Shinigami plot was drawing to a close. There was no hope of halting the devastation.

Kasey simply hoped she could do something to save some lives. Something had to be done to mitigate the disaster that was about to occur. The cost of each human death was twofold. Every life was precious, and every death strengthened their foe.

She had no doubt that Akihiro's lingering presence in the city was merely to steal the life force of its inhabitants as they expired. As the carnage unfolded around her, Kasey remembered her earlier visions. In them, the Shinigami's bastion, 432 Park Avenue had stood unmoved and undamaged. Strengthened by whatever preparations Akihiro had laid, it had seemed immune from the seismic activity. As lives by the thousands had been lost, their lifeforce had run up the skyscraper, the building itself taking on a sickly tinge of green.

She'd seen the same transference of energy when John had died at the Shinigami's hand. The thought made her dry heave. The enormity of the Akihiro's callousness still overwhelmed her.

Raising her gaze, she saw her destination come into view. She was at the southernmost point of Manhattan. She ran to the city's edge and grasped the steel rail as she looked out over the bay.

The dark waters had a green tinge to them. Whether it was her imagination or an actual result of the subterranean chaos, she didn't know.

A deafening explosion rang out behind her as the earth reeled beneath her feet. Stumbling, Kasey fell to the ground. Pain shot up her arms as the abrasive surface of the sidewalk skinned both her palms. Kasey was thrown onto her back as the earth shook once more.

*This is it. The Shinigami device had been detonated.*

If Vida's prediction was accurate, it was already too late. The monolithic detonation far beneath Manhattan would have vaporized the Serpentinite deposits. The vast chasms created would undermine the city and reduce it to ruin.

The earth shook for what felt like an eternity. From flat on her back, Kasey couldn't tell how many buildings had been laid low. Fortunately, those nearest to her managed to stay upright, at least for the time being—likely a result of their distance from

Park Avenue. Kasey had run as far as her legs could take her and had reached the southern point of the island in the nick of time.

It wasn't a bid to escape her fate. She intended to stand against what would come next.

As the tremors ceased, she struggled to her feet. Her body roared its pained protest at the abuse it had suffered over the recent weeks.

*Not much longer now. It will all be over soon.*

As she teetered on her feet, she grabbed the steel rail for support. She looked over the rail into the murky depths of the bay. The water was already receding. The inky black waters rolled away from Manhattan like it was low tide. The water couldn't escape the city quick enough and as Kasey watched it recede, she knew Vida was right.

*Damn him. He's always right.*

The seconds ticked inexorably by, each one coming and going as the city burned to ashes behind her. She couldn't worry about that now. The worst still lay ahead.

Then she saw it. At first, against the horizon, it was almost indiscernible among the angry storm clouds that blended seamlessly with the sea beneath. As it rolled toward Kasey, she could see it clearer and clearer with each passing moment. The wall of water was almost a hundred feet high, racing toward the city.

This was the implacable, crushing conclusion to the Shinigami plot.

The immense wall of water would be the end of New York City. It would sweep through the structurally weakened cityscape doing incalculable damage. Anyone on the street would be drowned or battered to death by the debris.

It was even larger than Kasey had imagined. As the wall of water rolled toward her, she realized the impossibility of her task.

What was one woman against such a wave? It was a tsunami, the likes of which the East Coast had never seen.

Kasey raised her hands and summoned her magic. Anything she could do to slow the tide would save lives. It wasn't a matter of if the wave would strike the city, but simply how far it would reach. Every block it rolled through, it would claim thousands, if not tens of thousands of lives.

The sting of her defeat was bitter, but if she could rob Akihiro of even a single life force it was worth it to her.

She had seen too much suffering and felt too much pain to let another person endure the heartache she had struggled with every day. As the wave closed, Kasey felt a vibration in her pocket. It was her phone.

Somehow with all the damage the city had suffered, her cellular service was still working. As the wave plunged toward her, Kasey ripped out her phone. The display read *Mom*.

Saying goodbye was more than Kasey could bear. She rejected the call. The cell display flashed back to its desktop.

It read 15th of December 2017 5:35 PM.

Kasey looked up. As the wave descended, so did a thick gray-green mist. The familiar embrace of her prescience enshrouded her as her vision closed.

She was out of time.

**Join Kasey as she fights for her life in *Until My Dying Day*.**

# ABOUT THE AUTHOR

Sam is a writer of magically-charged fantasy adventures. His passion for action, magic and intrigue spawned his Arcanoverse—a delightfully deluded universe that blends magic, myth, and the modern world in a melting pot that frequently explodes.

When he isn't hiding away in his writing cave, his favorite hobbies include cooking, indulging sugary cravings, gaming, and trying to make his children laugh. You can find more of his work at www.samuelcstokes.com or connect with him at the links below.

a   amazon.com/S-C-Stokes/e/B0161CBT5U

f   facebook.com/SCStokesOfficial

g   goodreads.com/author/show/3043773.S_C_Stokes

BB  bookbub.com/authors/s-c-stokes

# ALSO BY S.C. STOKES

## Conjuring A Coroner Series

A Date With Death

Dying To Meet You

Life Is For The Living

When Death Knocks

One Foot In The Grave

One Last Breath

Until My Dying Day

A Taste Of Death

A Brush With Death

A Dance With Death

Death Warmed Up

Death Sentence

## Magical Midlife Crisis Series

Bounty Hunter Down Under

A Bay Of Angry Fae

Ghosts At The Coast

## Urban Arcanology Series

Half-Blood's Hex

Half-Blood's Bargain

Half-Blood's Debt

Half-Blood's Birthright

Half-Blood's Quest

## A Kingdom Divided Series

A Coronation Of Kings

When The Gods War

A Kingdom In Chaos

Bones Of The Fallen

A Siege Of Lost Souls

Made in United States
North Haven, CT
13 May 2023

36511672R10114